# BEWARE!!
# DO NOT READ THIS
# BOOK FROM
# BEGINNING TO END!

It's vacation time! Your family is going to WoodsWorld cabins. All the kids say terrifying creatures roam the woods there at night — werewolves, trolls, and hideous monsters. But you're not scared. Until your mom makes nerdy Todd Morris come along. And until Todd insists that the two of you must brave the dark woods on the night of the full moon to find his stolen treasure. Can you survive until sunrise — alive?

The scary adventure is all about you. You decide what will happen. And you decide how terrifying the scares will be.

Start on page 1. Then follow the instructions at the bottom of each page. You make the choices.

If you make the right choices, you will escape the werewolves of WoodsWorld. If you make the wrong choice . . . BEWARE!

So take a long, deep breath, cross your fingers, and turn to page 1 to GIVE YOURSELF GOOSE-BUMPS!

READER BEWARE —
YOU CHOOSE THE SCARE!

Look for more
GIVE YOURSELF GOOSEBUMPS adventures
from R.L. STINE

#1 Escape From the Carnival of Horrors
#2 Tick Tock, You're Dead!
#3 Trapped in Bat Wing Hall
#4 The Deadly Experiments of Dr. Eeek

# R.L. STINE
## GIVE YOURSELF

## NIGHT IN WEREWOLF WOODS

AN
**APPLE**
PAPERBACK

SCHOLASTIC INC.
New York Toronto London Auckland Sydney

A PARACHUTE PRESS BOOK

ISBN 0-590-67319-X

12 11 10 9 8 7 6 5 4 3 2 1                    6 7 8 9/9 0 1/0

Printed in the U.S.A.                                            40

First Scholastic Printing, April 1996

"Nerd Alert! Nerd Alert!"

We interrupt your perfect summer vacation at Deep Woods Lake to bring you this special Nerd News: Your parents have invited their best friends, Mr. and Mrs. Morris, and their super-nerd son, Todd, to share the cabin with your family this year! You can't believe it. Your worst *nerdmare* has just come true.

"This can't be happening to me!" you say aloud as your family's minivan pulls up to WoodsWorld. You've already spotted the Morrises' car. It's parked beneath a string of colored lanterns hanging over the entrance to WoodsWorld. Woods-World is the cabin community that your family has vacationed at every summer since you were a baby.

Then you spot Todd. He's gawky, stringy-haired, and wears thick black-rimmed glasses.

"Hey! Hey! What do you say?" Todd calls to you. His big hand whirly-birds out of the car window in a nerdy wave.

"Be nice," your mom cautions.

"Yes, maybe Todd is different now," says your dad.

"Oh, he's different, all right," you moan. "From everyone else on this whole planet!"

---

*Go to PAGE 2.*

Your minivan and the Morrises' car both roll up the gravel drive next to Evergreen Cabin. You gaze around. Nothing has changed since last summer. The woods behind your cabin are still dark and deep. The sparkling blue lake in front of the cabin is as smooth as glass. A narrow, sandy beach stretches into an easy curve around the shoreline of the lake.

The sun has almost set, leaving behind a fiery pink-orange glow in the sky. There's enough daylight left for you to notice a note taped to the screen door of your cabin.

"Cool!" you cry. You jump out of the car. "That must be a note from my friends," you tell your parents. You sprint across the lawn and up the porch steps. You pull the note off the cabin door.

*To read what the note says, turn to PAGE 3.*

You unfold the note. You read it out loud, "Kids-only campfire tonight — eight P.M. at the beach."

"Wonderful!" your mom cries, as she hurries up behind you. "It's only seven o'clock now. You can help unload the car and then go. This will be a perfect opportunity for the other WoodsWorld kids to meet Todd."

"And a perfect opportunity for them to think I'm a nerd, too, because I'm with him," you mutter. But no one hears you. Your parents and Mr. and Mrs. Morris have gone inside the cabin.

You watch Todd unload his stuff from the car. As he pulls out a red tin box, three very large, red-haired boys bike up your driveway. They're the Murphy brothers — Jess, Buck, and Sharky.

"Welcome to WoodsWorld, Nerdo," the oldest brother, Sharky, taunts Todd. Sharky is fifteen. He looks as if he has been lifting weights since he was two years old. Last summer a kid told you that Sharky got his nickname because "getting into a fight with Sharky is like trying to survive a shark attack."

"I see you brought us a present," Sharky says to Todd. He grabs the tin box and tosses it to his youngest brother, Jess.

"Hey!" Todd shouts. "That's my pewter figure collection! Bring that box back!" Tears form in his eyes as the Murphy brothers pedal away, taking the box with them.

---

*Go to PAGE 12.*

It's a cave!

"In all the summers I've been coming to WoodsWorld," you say to Todd, "I never knew there was a cave here. Let's check it out."

Then you hear a voice from somewhere deep in the cave. A voice calling *your* name.

You think the voice sounds like Sharky Murphy, but you can't be sure. "Hello?" you answer. You start to move forward into the deep black cave.

Todd tugs you back. "Don't go in," he warns.

Again the voice from inside calls your name.

You feel pulled by the voice and pulled by Todd at the same time. What's it going to be? Go in or stay out?

*To answer the call of the cave, turn to PAGE 81.*

*If you'd feel safer listening to Todd and staying out of the cave, go to PAGE 37.*

"Done!" the troll's voice booms in your head. Instantly you feel your arms begin to bulge with super-strength. For the second time tonight, you are turning into a super muscle-bound kid. The transformation is complete. Your whole body is muscles on top of muscles on top of muscles.

The padlock breaks off with hardly a turn of your hand. *Rrrrrrrip!* You tear down the heavy library door.

Uh-oh! The noise brings your parents running to see what's going on. Get out of here fast, so the troll doesn't get them too!

*If you duck into the library, go to PAGE 131.*
*If you head for the woods, race to PAGE 73.*

# 6

You can't help feeling sorry for Todd. You decide to take him to the campfire. "Maybe if those Murphy brothers see you crying, they'll feel sorry for you, too," you tell Todd.

"They are the meanest boys I've ever met," Todd wails. He takes a package of tissues out of his shorts pocket and blows his nose. Loud!

"Really, Todd!" you say. "You'll scare them with that honking more than they could ever scare you!"

"I just want my pewter collection back. It's my most precious possession." As soon as Todd says this, the faucets open again. He can't stop crying. "I can't go to the campfire," he sobs. "My sinuses are all clogged now. You'll have to face them alone, I guess."

"Alone?" you repeat, cheering up immediately. "Without you, Todd?"

"I'm sorry," Todd weeps. "I just don't feel like going to a party tonight."

"If you insist!" you say happily.

*Go to PAGE 9.*

You keep your eyes closed. Your body relaxes. You start to feel so light, so calm, so . . .

You open your eyes wide. What happened?

The bump against the cave wall must have really knocked you and Todd out. Whatever happened after that is a mystery to you both. You don't know how long you were lying in that pool of slime in that cave.

You gaze around. You're out of the cave now and sitting propped up against a big tree. The light of the full moon is shining directly on you and Todd.

Todd sits with his back to you. You look down and shriek!

There are hairy, clawed hands where your hands should be!

Then Todd turns his face toward you and smiles a fanged smile. You open your mouth to scream, but the only sound coming out is a sound you've heard before. . . .

*HOW-OW-OW-OWL!*

You remember Sharky's words: This is a perfect night for the werewolves of WoodsWorld to come out.

Sharky was right. No one is safe here. Not now. Not ever. The werewolves now have two new members of the pack — you and Todd. Break out the shaving cream. Things are looking pretty hairy now!

**THE END**

"Okay, Todd," you announce. You fold up the note and slip it into the pocket of your jeans. "This means war!"

"Yeah!" Todd agrees with a sudden burst of courage. He grips your arm and asks, "What werewolves? Where?"

"That's exactly what we're going to find out," you reply. You quickly fill Todd in on Sharky's story about the werewolves. You slip your sneakers back on as Todd pulls jeans over his Looney Tunes pajamas. Then, holding a flashlight in one hand and a nervous Todd in the other, you sneak out the front door.

Slowly, you and Todd creep down the porch steps. You step onto the grass and stop.

You hear rustling in the bushes near the cabin.

"Who's there?" you demand in a loud whisper.

The only answer is another haunting howl from somewhere deep in the woods. Clouds cover the full moon now, making it difficult to see the path.

You spot two sets of blinking lights in the distance. Two red lights blink in the direction of the path leading to the beach. Two white lights blink in the opposite direction, down a path that leads deep into the woods.

"Which way?" Todd asks, clinging to your arm.

*To investigate the red lights, turn to PAGE 75.*
*Check out the white lights, go to PAGE 30.*

You leave Todd to cry alone at the cabin. "You stay here and unpack your stuff," you say to Todd. "I'll go to the campfire and get the box back for you."

You hurry out the cabin door. You head for the usual campfire spot at the south end of the beach. A giant fire is already blazing when you arrive. You see your friend, Lauren Woods. Her parents own WoodsWorld. She and the regular crowd of WoodsWorld kids are sitting around the fire listening to Sharky Murphy tell a creepy story.

". . . remember the legend of the werewolves," Sharky is saying mysteriously. "At first you may think you are talking to a friend. Then, when the full moon comes out from behind a cloud, you'll see hair begin to grow on your friend's face. Fangs take the place of teeth. A voice that once was human turns to a beastly howl." Sharky pauses and lowers his voice to a whisper. "Look!" he says. "The full moon is out tonight. This is a perfect night for the werewolves of WoodsWorld to appear. No one is safe here. Not now. Not *ever*."

*Go to PAGE 28.*

As you sink deeper into the quicksand, you see Todd being transformed by the moonlight.

Hair grows on his face and hands. His teeth lengthen into wolflike fangs. With flashing red eyes, Todd turns toward you. He opens his mouth and lets out a bloodcurdling, hungry *HOW-OW-OW-OWL!*

"Todd!" you shout. "Turn your face away from the moonlight! Don't look at the full moon! It's a werewolf moon! Don't let it get you!"

You try one more time to pull your feet free. This time the quicksand's grip loosens! In one swift move you leap from the hole and throw yourself at Todd. The force of your body moves him out of the moon's light.

You hold Todd down. The beam of moonlight slowly disappears as a cloud passes over the full moon. As the light goes away, so do Todd's werewolf features.

"That's it!" you exclaim. "Now I understand what we have to do."

*Turn to PAGE 78.*

A hideous laugh erupts from the man's fanged mouth. His eyes flash a brighter red, spotlighting a face covered with coarse werewolf hair. Clawed, hairy hands reach for your neck as the man growls, "Yes! I am one of them! And soon you will be one of them, too!"

He opens his fanged mouth to bite you. Suddenly you spot two buttons by the elevator door. One reads *STOP!* and the other reads *GO!* You stretch out your index finger and press one.

*If you press* STOP*! turn to PAGE 21.*
*If you press* GO*! turn to PAGE 29.*

You try to pretend that you don't see Todd crying. But this kid is not a quiet sniffler. He's a loud sobber!

"Boo hoo! Boo hoo!" Todd cries. Tears spurt out of his eyes like a water main break in the middle of Main Street.

"All right, all right!" you finally say. "I'll go to the campfire and get your precious pewter collection back."

"I'm coming, too," Todd says. He wipes his nose on his sleeve. Gross!

You glance over at the porch. The parents are so busy talking, they don't notice that Todd's tears are flooding the place. You notice though. Now you have to decide if you're going to bring Todd to the campfire or leave him to cry at the cabin.

If you decide to ditch Todd and go to the campfire alone, turn to PAGE 9.

If you decide to drag Todd with you to the campfire, go to PAGE 6.

A promise is a promise. You promised Todd you would get his box back tonight. You decide you have to go into the woods. Alone.

"It's no big deal," you think to yourself. "I've been coming to WoodsWorld forever. I've never seen werewolves here before."

You follow the Murphys up a gravel path to the woods. You hope they will lead you to the box. The only problem is the Murphys are nowhere in sight. They have sprinted up the path in the darkness. You peer ahead, but see nothing.

The full moon is behind a cloud. Total darkness surrounds you like a thick blanket. The woods are silent tonight. Even the raccoons and other night creatures seem to have gone to bed already. Nothing is out here. "Nothing except me," you say softly to yourself.

*HOW-OW-OW-OW-OWL!*

You whirl around. What made that horrible noise?

You glance to your right. And then to your left. Nothing.

You continue along the path. The gravel crunches under your sneakers. And then you see it! A light flickering up ahead!

*Go to PAGE 106*.

"Aaaaachooo!" Todd sneezes. The werewolf's fur makes Todd's allergies act up instantly.

"Gesundheit!"

Todd looks at you. Then at Lauren. "What did you say?" he asks.

"I said, 'Gesundheit,' " a deep, growling voice answers.

Todd whirls around. "Huh?"

"Gesundheit," the werewolf repeats. "I was speaking in German. Instead of saying bless you, I said Gesundheit."

You and Lauren inch back behind a huge tree. "What happened to the werewolf?" she whispers. "Now he's talking like we talk!"

"The SMARTS BOX," you whisper back. "Those O's must do a lot more than just fill a person's head with facts. Anyone who eats it gets good manners! The werewolf is talking just like a polite human being would!"

Go to PAGE 49.

*HOW-OW-OW-OW-OWL!* You hear the were-wolves howl in the not-too-distant distance.

"Ohhhh!" Todd moans, as the pterodactyl flies up and out of the pit. The flying reptile tips sideways. It drops you and Todd on the ground right by the werewolves.

You land right in front of the werewolves' feet. The wolves are pacing and circling. Some are on all four legs. Some are standing upright on two hind legs. Their growls and howls bounce off the walls of the cave and hit your ears like a pair of cymbals clashing.

Whew! What an odor these wolves give off! You have never smelled anything so bad in your life!

A hand on your shoulder causes you to spin around. You are face to face with . . . and you really can't believe this . . . !

*Go to PAGE 20.*

You're sure it is a smart idea to capture the werewolf. You remember all the old ape movies on TV. King Kong was captured! Mighty Joe Young was captured! And now you will carry on the tradition when you capture this werewolf! Scientists will be grateful to you. You'll be famous. And besides, how else can you prove you really saw one?

The hairy beast is still sniffing at the cereal on the ground. It shouldn't be too difficult to trap it.

"Throw me your sweatshirt," you call to Todd. Your super-smart mind has already figured out how to use the sweatshirt to blind the werewolf. "While the werewolf is sniffing the O's, we'll catch it," you whisper.

"But what about finding my box?" Todd complains.

"Never mind that now," you say. You stand behind the werewolf. It's clearly interested in only one thing now — eating the red O's.

Todd stands next to you. He is ready to help in the capture. "I'll count to three," you explain. "Then we'll grab the werewolf. One, two . . ."

*Go to PAGE 70.*

"I did it!" you shout. You're amazed at your power. With no trouble at all you lift the surprised werewolf in the air — just by the strength of one finger!

And just to teach the werewolf a lesson, you twirl it around in the air above your head. Then you fling the beast far, far into the woods. Your super strength did the job!

"*HOW-OW-OW-OW-OW-OW-OW-OWL!*" cries the airborne werewolf all the way into the dark woods.

"You really do have super strength!" Todd cries. "You have all the power now!"

*Go to PAGE 31.*

You decide to turn back and face the werewolf. You could easily handle one or two of these horrible red fire ants. But *thousands* of them are running for your ankles!

"Come on, let's get out of here!" you shout to Lauren and Todd.

With you in the lead, the three of you turn back on the path and run. This time you run right into a snarling, growling werewolf. The moon suddenly appears from behind a cloud. The face of the werewolf is captured by the moonlight. You see its filthy fur drenched in thick, slimy drool. Its long, red tongue licks its fangs. It stands on two hind legs. Its clawed front paws reach for you.

"The werewolf!" Todd cries. "I knew we should have stayed where we were."

The werewolf turns to Todd. A disgusting-looking red foam dribbles from its mouth and drips down its ragged fur. You can smell Cherry-O's on the werewolf's breath. It moves closer to Todd. Closer.

"Help!" Todd screams.

*Go to PAGE 14.*

"Forget this!" you cry. "I'm out of here!"

You decide you're going back to the cabin to get help. It's one thing to try to get Todd's stupid box back. It's a whole other thing to be eaten alive by bats!

You quickly turn to leave. But in the darkness and with the bats flapping around your eyes, you can't see where you're going. You try to retrace your steps out of the cave. But you are blocked by what seems to be a wall of ice.

You feel the frozen wall with your hands. The surface is so cold it burns. You quickly pull back your hands. Then you hear a strange rumble.

The ice wall starts to move!

It slides open like a sliding glass door. You see a small room completely covered in ice. A blast of arctic air rushes out at you. The warmer air from the rest of the cave surges through the ice door. A perfectly round ice window in the roof of the room melts.

Light from the full moon outside streams in through the newly formed skylight. The moon shines on the frozen forms of thirteen gruesome werewolves.

Oh, no! The frozen werewolves are beginning to melt!

*Go to PAGE 109.*

# 20

You rub your eyes to make sure you're not seeing things that aren't really there. But you're not. What you think you see really is there. And what a shock — all three Murphy brothers, right here, inside the cave!

"Well, that explains the smell in here!" you whisper to Todd. "It isn't the werewolves. It's the Murphys who smell!"

You see the Murphys, but they don't see you. They're too busy defending themselves from the werewolves. Jess is holding a rock and is ready to heave it if the werewolves come too close.

Suddenly one wolf leaps forward. It pushes all three Murphy brothers into the center of the pack of werewolves.

You've never seen the Murphys look so scared. They don't look like bullies now. Now they look like regular kids. Regular terrified kids, that is.

For a second you think, Well, it serves them right! They're the ones who got us into this mess. But in the next second you feel kind of sorry for them.

Decisions, decisions. What will you do? Try to help the Murphys, or let the werewolves have them?

*Lend a helping hand on PAGE 84.*
*Throw the Murphys to the wolves on PAGE 87.*

# STOP!

Congratulations. You have chosen to STOP this story just when you were about to be turned into one of *them*. But what are *they*?

Elevator operators in the Bottomless Pit Elevator!

If you had not stopped the story at this point, you would have had nowhere to go but down. There's only one thing worse than a bad ending, and that's no ending. So consider your choice wise because it brings you to what is officially known here as

**THE END**

## 22

Another low growl fills the cave.

Todd looks as surprised and afraid as you are.

"No," Todd says in answer to your question. "That wasn't me. Was it you?"

The growling sound is louder now. Louder and closer.

"No! It wasn't me!" you reply.

The full moon's beam suddenly breaks through the crack in the cave's ceiling. The cloud has passed by and the moonlight is as clear and bright as a Hollywood spotlight.

This time it is not shining on Todd's face.

It shines on another face. And another.

Two faces that are not quite human. Faces that are transforming before your very eyes into snarling, growling wolves. *Werewolves*, to be more exact. What should you do?

---

*Your knowledge of the GOOSEBUMPS book* The Werewolf of Fever Swamp *will help you decide what to do.*

*What type of bird did the Werewolf of Fever Swamp rip apart?*

*If you think it was a cardinal, go to PAGE 57.*

*If you think it was a heron, turn to PAGE 68.*

You thought you were alone, floating in the darkness. And you thought your own breathing was the only sound around. But now, right next to your ear, you hear other breathing. Air is being sucked in and blown out. Air in. Air out.

You strain your ears to listen better. You hold your own breath so you won't confuse it with this new sound.

Yes. It is breathing. Slow, even, steady, deep breathing.

Air in. Air out. Air in. Air out.

The rhythm is as regular as a sleeping giant's breathing.

But in the darkness you see nothing. Your eyes are no help to your ears now. All you can do is listen.

Air in. Air out. Air in. Your own breathing begins to join in the rhythm.

---

*Air in. Air out. Keep breathing and go to PAGE 113.*

"It's a werewolf!" Todd yells in horror.

Lauren covers her eyes and screams, "I can't look!"

The darkness makes it impossible to see clearly. And you're afraid to turn your flashlight on the beast. You can just barely make out the form of the werewolf. It's standing on all four legs.

Todd and Lauren are cornered by the beast. They are screaming for help. The werewolf hasn't spotted you yet. You have no weapons. What can you do?

But wait! You've got it! The boxes! Maybe one of the boxes will help you!

If you open the SMARTS BOX, maybe you will be able to figure out a genius plan to defeat the werewolf. But, then again, if you are SUPER STRONG, you can fight the werewolf and win. Which box should you open first?

*If you choose the* SMARTS BOX, *hurry to PAGE 50.*

*If you choose the* SUPER-STRENGTH BOX, *go to PAGE 95.*

Ask Todd and Lauren for advice? Forget it! They saw what the SUPER-STRENGTH cereal did for you. Now they're both gobbling up a handful of it, too. In seconds Todd and Lauren have both turned into muscle-bound hulks. The three of you show off your giant muscles for each other.

"This is *so* cool!" Lauren exclaims. She lifts a huge boulder without even straining.

"Power!" Todd declares, raising a fallen tree trunk above his head.

"Hahahahahahahahahaha!" The evil laughter of the menacing troll fills the woods. You cover your ears to keep out the awful sound.

The troll has had just about enough of you three now. He puckers up his thick, blubbery lips and whistles. Instantly, Lauren drops the boulder. Todd drops the tree trunk.

"Roll over!" the troll orders.

Todd and Lauren fall to the ground and roll over. Their super strength has been zapped. But how?

*Find out on PAGE 66.*

You are strong enough — and smart enough — to resist the trance! When you are out of the troll's sight, you reach your fingers up to your ears — and pull out a SUPER-STRENGTH O from each ear!

"That's better," you say. "Now I can hear again." Plugging your ears with *O*'s so you wouldn't hear the troll's whistle worked! Without his whistle, the troll is powerless. After your muscles disappeared, you plugged up your ears with the *O*'s. Then you just pretended to obey his command.

"Come back!" Todd cries out again.

"That's exactly what I plan to do," you say softly to yourself. Quietly, you tiptoe back up the path to where the troll has just changed his size to mini-troll. He is perched on a branch of a low shrub. He speaks right into Todd's and Lauren's ears. "You will be in my absolute power forever," the troll says to his two captives. "With or without the *O*'s, I can control your every move with my voice!" He puckers up his lips and prepares to whistle.

Lauren sees you sneaking up behind the troll. You put a finger to your lips and signal her to keep quiet.

*Go to PAGE 53.*

Then you see the thing that started this trouble — the red tin box. Buck was telling the truth. The werewolves do have the box.

"Todd, look!" you cry out. You point to the box resting at the feet of the fiercest werewolf.

"My pewter collection!" Todd exclaims when he sees the box. He forgets for the moment that danger is only inches away. The werewolves' tongues hang out between pointed oversized teeth. The smell of their hot breath makes you feel sick.

The pterodactyl from the Bottomless Pit swoops past you. The flapping of its wings sends dust and dirt flying up from the ground. The werewolves tuck their faces under their fur-covered arms, trying to keep the clouds of dirt out of their red eyes.

While the werewolves' heads are buried in their arms, you and Todd crawl between their hairy legs. You grab the red tin box. Then you sprint to a corner, out of the wolves' immediate sight.

"Got it!" you cry, clutching the box to your chest.

*Turn to PAGE 124.*

Sharky laughs an evil laugh as he finishes his story. The kids sitting around the campfire study each other's faces — searching for hair or maybe fangs.

As clouds cover the full moon, the campfire party breaks up. Everyone says good-night. Lauren Woods laughs as she calls to you, "Nighty-night, don't let the werewolves bite!"

"Did you ever see a werewolf, Sharky?" one of the younger kids asks before he leaves.

"Ha!" laughs Sharky. "My brothers and I saw plenty of werewolf tracks in the woods just before we came to this campfire. Isn't that right, Jess?"

"Yeah," the youngest Murphy brother says. "We saw the wolf tracks when we were burying that nerdy kid's box."

So, you think to yourself, they buried Todd's box. But where?

You promised to get the box back for Todd. But should you go out alone tonight when the moon is full?

*If you decide to look for the box tonight, turn to PAGE 13.*

*If you decide to go back to the cabin, turn to PAGE 71.*

# GO!

Well, that sure took a lot of courage on your part! Nobody ever pushes GO! when a clawed hairy hand is reaching over to grab his or her neck. But, guess what? You pushed GO! And now you and Todd are both GOing to have the ride of your life on the Bottomless Pit Elevator.

But wait! The elevator door slides open. The elevator is stuck! You have a second chance. Do something — fast!

"One, two, three, jump!" you cry, as you pull Todd out the door. Holding on to each other, you and Todd begin to fall.

Down, down deeper and deeper into the pit.

You pick up speed. Your ears start to pop as your body plunges faster and faster. Your body flips upside down. Everything is spinning.

And then a sharp ringing sound pierces your ears!

*Turn to PAGE 52.*

You decide to take the path through the woods that leads to the white lights.

"Please hurry," Todd begs you. "I need my box back. Those pewter figures are like my best friends."

"We'll get them back or my name isn't Phineas Z. Smeltzenseltzer!" you say.

"But your name isn't Phineas Z. Smeltzenseltzer," Todd answers. He misses the joke completely.

"Oh, brother!" you sigh. "Come on, Todd. Let's follow this path." You start to hike into the woods. The path is lined with a wall of thick, dark bushes.

"Two lights probably mean double trouble," Todd warns. He follows too closely behind you. He keeps stepping on your heels.

"More like triple trouble when you're dealing with the Murphy brothers," you add. You don't really care about Todd's box. But you don't think the bullies should wreck anyone's vacation at WoodsWorld. Not even nerdy Todd's vacation.

A strange noise ahead on the path catches your and Todd's attention. It sounds like twigs cracking.

"What's that?" Todd asks, clinging to your arm.

*Find out on PAGE 132.*

"Not so fast," says a scratchy little voice from out of nowhere. "I am the one with all the power here!"

You all gasp when you see who's talking. A troll no more than one and a half feet high. He is standing on a rock with his tiny feet apart, fists curled, and a smirk on a wart-filled green face.

"I am the Master of the Box! Whoever eats from the SUPER-STRENGTH BOX is my servant!" The troll stares right at you with his beady black eyes. Then he laughs in your face. "Ha! You think you have power, pipsqueak? That beast you just hurled was nothing but a small dog until I fed him my magic O's. I have the power. Only I have it! Bow down to your master, slave!"

"I'm not your slave!" you fire back at him. You flex the muscles on your arms. Your arms now look like a mountain range. "I could flatten you in a second!"

You could. But will you?

*If you ask Todd and Lauren for advice, go to PAGE 25.*

*If you choose to grab a nearby branch and swat the troll, go to PAGE 56.*

"YIIIIIIIIIIIIIIIIIIIIIIIIIIIIIIIIIIIIIIKES!" you scream.

A huge pack of werewolves moving at top speed burst on the scene. They are half-man, half-wolf. Foam slides from their open mouths. Bits of leftovers from the most recent victims hang from their fangs and claws. There is no doubt in your mind. You will be their next victim.

You quickly aim the flashlight beam directly at them. Maybe you can blind the wolves for a minute with your light. Now you can see the whole pack clearly. And all their red eyes are on one thing — *you*. You're still holding on to the SMARTS BOX.

"Of course!" you cry. You reach into the box and shove some cereal into your mouth. You swallow a few *O*'s and immediately feel like a genius.

"Now that you're so smart," Lauren says, "what should we do?"

*Use your brain and go to PAGE 126.*

The werewolves are too close. You have to start howling. It's your only hope.

*"HOW-OW-OW-OWL!"*

*"HOW-OW-OW-OWL!"*

*"HOW-OW-OW-OWL!"*

*"HOW-OW-OW-OWL!"*

*"HOW-OW-OW-OWL!"*

*"HOW-OW-OW-OWL!"*

You and Todd take turns howling to keep the werewolves away. You have been standing here howling for hours. So far it's working. There is not a werewolf in sight! Good job! Keep up the howling until . . .

**THE END**

"Honey?" you hear your mom's voice. "Honey, you've been sleeping for hours. Are you feeling all right?"

You open your eyes and look around for Todd.

"Where is he? Where is Todd?" you ask your mother.

"Todd is asleep, too. I had to wake you finally to tell you that the Morrises and Dad and I are going to play tennis. Can you and Todd stay out of trouble while we're gone?"

"Oh, Mom," you assure her, "don't worry. What kind of trouble could we possibly get into at WoodsWorld?"

"You're right," your mom says. "Okay, then. See you later."

She leaves and you lie in bed thinking of all the events of the night before. Was it all a weird dream? That's it. It must have been a dream. You close your eyes for a few more minutes and hear a familiar voice.

"Hey! Hey! What do you say!"

It is Todd's same goofy-sounding voice. But when you open one eye you see a hairy, scary werewolf standing in the doorway wearing Todd's pajamas! Oh, no! If this is not a bad dream, you sure hope it is

**THE END**

You decide to take on the army of red fire ants.
"I've got an idea," you announce. You swat a large ant off your arm and turn to Todd. "Here, hold this SMARTS BOX while I feed the ants some of these Cherry-O's from it."

You grab a handful of O's out of the box. Then you scatter most of them at the base of the ant-filled tree trunk. You put the remaining cereal in your pocket.

"It's working!" Lauren exclaims. "The ants are all heading straight for the O's!"

Sure enough, all the red fire ants are crawling off your bodies and over to the O's. Thousands of tiny mouths crunch and munch through the pile of cereal.

Then you have an even better idea. You're going to slam your foot down on the whole hungry colony, squashing them once and for all. You raise one foot above the obvious leaders of the group. But before you stomp them out, you stop. Something strange is going on.

The ants are turning their tiny faces up to you. They are making strange motions with their little arms!

*Go to PAGE 59.*

"Hey, look at me! I'm strong!" Sharky cries.

"Me, too!" Buck exclaims. He pushes an enormous fist in Todd's face.

"Me three," Jess says, testing his new strength by lifting Todd up.

"HELP!" Todd screams high above Jess's head.

"Hey, Sharky," you call over to the biggest brother. "I give up. You win. You can have Todd and this jumping box."

"What!" Todd hollers. "You can't leave me with them!"

You toss Sharky the jumping box with the troll still inside.

Jess puts Todd down. He hurries over to Sharky and Buck. Sharky starts to open the box.

At that moment you catch Lauren and Todd's attention. You give them a let's-get-out-of-here look. Then the three of you make a run for it.

When you are far enough away, you glance back and see exactly what you were hoping you would see.

*Go to PAGE 114.*

"All right, all right," you snap at Todd as he pulls you back from the mouth of the cave. "We won't go in the cave. But do you want your box back or not?"

"Of course I do," he says, still holding on to you. "But I think I'm allergic to caves. I feel kind of strange."

"Well, I feel kind of strange, too, with you holding on to me all the time!" You shake his hand off your arm and step back. Ooops! Instantly your feet sink into a thick, mucky goo that won't let go. Quicksand!

You're glued to the spot and sinking deeper and deeper.

"Hey, Todd," you cry. "Get me out of this, will you?"

But Todd isn't listening. He has his back turned. He is staring at a beam of light shining through a crack in the cave's ceiling. Todd gazes up and shouts, "I see the full moon!"

"Never mind the full moon, Todd," you beg him. "Please, pull me out of here!"

Todd does nothing. You quickly check and see that Todd isn't standing in quicksand. But he can't seem to move either. He stares motionless at the light of the full moon. Todd is in a trance!

*Turn to PAGE 10.*

This falling thing is starting to get boring. With no bottom to this pit, there's nothing to look forward to.

Since there's nothing to see down below, you and Todd gaze up instead. You immediately are hit in the eye with drops of some liquid.

"Yikes!" Todd screams. "There's a whole pack of those werewolves up there!"

Todd's right. At the rim of the pit, twenty or more hungry werewolves are leaning into the hole. Those drops that hit you in the eye were drops of drool dripping from the fangs of the hairy beasts.

Gross! The werewolves want food, and you and Todd are it. You can feel their fire-red eyes staring right at you.

A hot glob of drool hits the tip of Todd's ear and dribbles down the side of his neck.

"Oh, *disgusting*!" he moans. He pulls his hand away from your arm to wipe off the steaming drool. Uh-oh. Todd is falling away from you. You're both on your own now.

*Go to PAGE 102.*

The woods are alive with the sounds of trolls' whistles. If you could hear it, you would be deafened by it.

They whistle louder and louder and louder. Soon the sound of their own whistle drives them crazy. They all hold their own ears as they spin around and around like tiny troll tops. They're out of control! While trying to control you, they have lost all control of themselves.

Right before your eyes you see hundreds of trolls disappearing into the ground. The faster they spin, the deeper into the ground they go. Soon all of them are right where you want them — GONE!

You stand up and brush the dirt from your clothes. Then you stroll back to your cabin, whistling as you go.

**THE END**

"Ugh!" you cry. "Disgusting!"

The trolls turn on you. All at once the whole horrible population of the creepy little creatures starts whistling. *"Tweeeet! Tweeeet! Tweeeeet! Tweeeeeeeet!"*

Your ears ache. The trolls' whistling begins to shrink your super-strength muscles.

"We've got the offender!" shouts the ugliest troll of all. Thick, lizard-skin eyelids droop down over his bulging green eyes. "Everyone attack! Attack the one who insults us!"

All your strength is gone. You are an easy target for the attacking trolls. They leap from trees and rocks. They land all over you. You fall to the ground. A tribe of trolls quickly crisscrosses your body with ropes, anchoring you to the spot.

"We've captured the giant!" the trolls cry.

What should you do?

*If you need more time to think, go to PAGE 94.*
*If you call for help, scream on PAGE 64.*

"Werewolves! There are werewolves behind you!" you finally manage to scream. "Jump, Todd, jump!"

You fumble with the faulty flashlight. This time it goes on. You point the flickering beam past Todd's slug-slimed head. You aim for the eyes of the snarling beasts. Yes! It's working!

"The light is hypnotizing them!" you shout. "Hurry! Jump across!"

"Oohhhhhh!" Todd cries, as he glances back and finds himself eyeball-to-eyeball with the werewolves.

"Jump!" you yell. "JUMP!"

As the werewolves reach out for him, Todd jumps. You lean over the edge of the gaping pit and grab for Todd's outstretched hand. You stretch your own arm as far as you can, and . . .

*If you catch Todd, turn to PAGE 80.*
*If you don't catch Todd, plunge to PAGE 61.*

Todd is standing next to you. He is just as surrounded by the beastly bats as you are. But Todd is acting as if they are butterflies instead of bats. He's even reaching out his hands to them!

A sudden gust of wind blows through the cave. The bats beat their wings furiously, which creates an instant whirlpool. The force pulls Todd backwards.

You can't believe your own eyes! Todd is being sucked into a tunnel — a tunnel filled with yellow bat eyes.

"Todd!" you scream.

"Bats! Bats! Everywhere, bats!" Todd yells, as you watch him being drawn deeper and deeper into the tunnel. "They're beautiful!"

You knew this kid was weird. Now what are you supposed to do?

Go down the Tunnel of Eyes after Todd? Or turn back and run for help?

*The eyes have it, if you turn to PAGE 47.*

*When the going gets tough, the tough get going . . . for help! Turn to PAGE 19.*

"I don't know where your box is," you answer Todd. "The troll has made Sharky so small now, I can't even hear his voice."

Smaller and smaller and smaller. Sharky, Jess, and Buck are shrinking right before your eyes.

"Yes!" the troll cries as he jumps around gleefully. "Now I have the information I need. The red tin box will be mine. I will be the master of another box in WoodsWorld."

You, Lauren, and Todd creep over toward the troll. You hide behind the bushes and watch. The troll is climbing a large maple tree. He quickly scales the trunk and scampers into the leafy branches.

"Aha! I found it!" the troll cries. "It's beautiful!"

"That's *my* box!" Todd whines.

"Sssssh," you whisper, gazing up at the tree. "I have a plan." You sneak over to the base of the tree. You grab hold of the trunk and shake. You shake the tree with all your might.

The troll hangs on to a branch. He swings back and forth. But Todd's red tin box falls to the ground. Todd snatches it up.

"Run!" you cry. You and your friends take off. "Run faster!" you shout, glancing back at the troll high in the tree. You head for your cabin at top speed, because you now know that what goes up, must always come down in

**THE END**

# 44

"Good evening," purrs a deep, velvety-smooth voice. "I've been expecting you."

"Expecting me? You have?" you gulp. You squint into the blackness, trying to see who is talking. But it is too dark.

"When the full moon is out, I always expect good things to come to my door," the voice says slowly.

"Maybe you can help me, doctor," you say nervously. "You see, I'm looking for a box that belongs to my friend. A red tin box. We've been searching all night, but we ran into some trouble."

"Trouble?" says the voice from the shadows.

"Wolves. Well, more like um . . . uh . . . werewolves to be exact," you explain.

"Werewolves, eh?" the deep voice says. The door opens wider. The doctor steps out into the light of the full moon. There's only one thing for you to do now — SCREAM!

*And go to PAGE 112.*

"Run!" you shout.

You take off, holding the boxes in your arms. You glance back to see if Lauren and Todd are following. It's so dark in the woods, you can't find your friends.

"We're right behind you," Lauren assures you.

"Run!" you shout again. Then your whole body smacks up against a tree trunk. "Oooff!" you gasp. The impact knocks the air right out of you.

"Ooooff!" Lauren adds, slamming into your back.

"Ooooff!" Todd cries. He plows into Lauren.

You feel the ache of sudden airlessness. But the ache instantly turns into a stinging feeling all over your legs, arms, neck, and face.

"Ouch! Ooo! Youch!" Todd screams. He jumps up and down, then rolls on the ground. "Red fire ants!"

*Hurry to PAGE 62.*

"Don't hurt us!" Buck begs the beast.

The werewolf snarls and lifts Buck up by his collar. Its hairy paws close around Buck's neck.

"Don't do it!" Lauren cries out.

Sharky and Jess Murphy are huddled together next to a tree. They have their eyes covered, but you see tears streaming down their cheeks. You've never seen the Murphys look so scared.

The werewolf ignores Lauren's plea. But then Todd speaks up. "Please don't hurt them," Todd says gently.

For a second it seems as if the werewolf is listening to Todd. But then it tightens its grip on Buck. The werewolf moves over to where Sharky and Jess stand shivering in their black high-top sneakers.

"GRRRRRRRRRRRRRRRR . . ." growls the werewolf, ready to finish off all three Murphys.

"You have to help us!" the Murphys cry.

---

*To help or not to help? That is the question! Turn to PAGE 91.*

You know you have to try to save Todd from the bats. Even if he doesn't realize he needs saving. Even if it means you have to face millions of bat faces yourself.

You step into the tunnel. You don't even try to fight the power of the tunnel's air currents. You let your body be sucked into the open mouth of the black hole. Immediately you hear the *THWAP* of flapping wings.

*THWAP! THWAP! THWAP!*

The sound is so close to your ears it's deafening. You flap your own arms back at the bats. This clears the way in front of you. Now you can see the choice you must make.

There are two more tunnels at the end of this tight-squeezing passageway. Above the sound of the bat wings, you hear the roaring of rushing waves of water. The sound is coming from the tunnel on the left.

And from the tunnel on the right comes a wicked howling that can only be one thing — wolves.

*To tackle the Tunnel of Waves, go to PAGE 51.*
*To brave the Tunnel of Wolves, go to PAGE 130.*

"Release my leg at once!" the troll demands. You open your hand, and he disappears completely. For a second you think you are free of his control.

*"Tweeeeet!"* comes his shrill whistle from behind you. At the sound of it you feel a renewed loss of power. "You must do what I tell you to do. You must get the red tin box for me. Inside the box there are enemies of the trolls," the troll declares. "I must have the box to control those enemies and protect the entire nation of trolls."

"There are other trolls?" you ask.

"Shhhh! The slave does not speak to the Master!" shouts the troll. "Where is the box? I command you to tell me now!"

"I don't have it," you say. "My friends and I are looking for it, too."

"Silence!" the troll sputters. "You must search everywhere for the box. Search the cabins. Search the WoodsWorld community center. Go now!"

*If you decide to search the cabins first, hurry to PAGE 76.*

*If you'd rather search the community center first, go to PAGE 60.*

You and Lauren stay hidden a little while longer. "My mother talks to our cat," Lauren says, "but your friend is actually talking to a werewolf!"

Todd and the talking werewolf are acting as if they have been friends for years. The red foam bubbling and frothing from the mouth of the werewolf doesn't seem to upset Todd at all.

"Here, take this," Todd says, handing the werewolf a tissue. "You've got gunk coming out of your mouth. Wipe it off."

The werewolf takes the tissue, wipes its mouth, and says, "Thank you, Todd."

"If only the Murphy brothers could act more like you," Todd declares. "You're so polite, and they are such beasts."

No sooner does Todd mention the word "beasts," than something horrible crashes through the bushes. Todd shrieks. The polite werewolf runs. You open your mouth to scream, too.

*If a scream comes out of your mouth, turn to* PAGE 32.

*If nothing comes out of your mouth, turn to* PAGE 119.

Smart move. You toss the SMARTS BOX to Todd. "Here, catch!" you shout.

Todd misses. The box falls to the ground, and the top flies open.

"I can't look!" Lauren cries, still hiding her eyes.

"Cereal!" Todd exclaims. "Cherry-O's!"

Sure enough, cherry-colored O's spill out of the box. The snarling werewolf's eyes light up when it sees food. It sniffs the ground where the O's spilled. Its fangs spear one. The werewolf pulls the O-shaped cereal out of its drooling mouth and stares at it. The werewolf can't seem to decide whether to eat it or play with it.

A piece of the SMARTS BOX cereal is lying on the ground near your foot. You pick it up, smell it, and pop it into your mouth. It tastes like ordinary Cherry-O's.

But as soon as you swallow it, you know there's nothing ordinary about this cereal. Your head feels strange. Ideas and thoughts fill your mind faster than you can blink.

What's happening to me? you wonder.

*Go to PAGE 103.*

*WHOOSH!*

You step into the Tunnel of Waves. A sudden flood of icy water forces you forward through the tight-fitting tunnel.

"Todd!" you scream over the roar of the waves. "Todd! Are you in here? TODD!"

A disgusting smell of rotten eggs fills your nostrils. "Sulfur, yeecchh!" you say to yourself. You remember the same horrible smell coming from the old mill pond at home. You try not to breathe it in as you scream out one more time, "TODD!"

No answer.

You gasp for fresh air from somewhere, anywhere. Then you struggle against the pounding pressure. A wall of waves pushes you from behind.

It's no use. You stop fighting the waves. Instead you stretch your arms out over your head and go with the flow.

Water fills your ears, your eyes, your mouth. The enormous, crashing waves carry your body through the tunnel. There is no end in sight!

*Float on to PAGE 67.*

The ringing is so loud, so horrible. The sound shatters the darkness. You have to stop the noise. Some way, any way. You can't stand it any longer.

You reach your arm out into the blackness . . .

. . . and shut off your alarm clock.

You slowly open your eyes. You look around. Where's Todd?

Then you realize you're at home, in your bed, clutching your pillow for dear life.

Your mother pushes open your bedroom door and pokes her head in. "Rise and shine! Today's the day we go to WoodsWorld."

"Really?" you ask. You need to make sure it truly was all a dream — the red tin box, the pit, the werewolves. "What time are we meeting Mr. and Mrs. Morris and Todd there?" you ask.

"What are you talking about?" your mother says. "The Morrises aren't coming with us. It's a family vacation — you, me, and Dad. Just like always."

You smile and lean back on your pillow. This just may turn out to be a fantastic summer in

**THE END**

In one quick motion you reach for the open SUPER-STRENGTH BOX. You throw it over the tiny troll. You stuff him into the box and close it tightly.

"Gotcha!" you cry triumphantly.

"No!" screams the troll from inside the box. "No! You can't do this to me! I am the Master of the Box! You'll be sorry. You will, you will! I'll get you for this!"

Lauren and Todd laugh at the sight of the box jiggling around on the ground. The little troll inside is rocking it back and forth.

"No! No! No!" he screams again.

What in the world are you going to do with a jumping box full of SUPER-STRENGTH O's and a mean little troll? Then the answer comes tramping through the bushes.

*Go to PAGE 97*.

"Gyzacck!"

"Gyzacck!"

"Gyzacck!"

Hey! What's going on here? It isn't the troll saying this weird word. It's Lauren and Todd and *you*!

You've run away from the troll, but before you left him he played a very mean trick. He stole all your vocabulary words and replaced them with just one word. Gyzacck!

You open your mouth to speak to Lauren. "Gyzacck!"

She opens her mouth to answer. "Gyzacck!"

And Todd cries, "Gyzacck!"

What does "Gyzacck" mean? Well, it can only mean one thing. For you and your friends this is

**GYZACCK!**

"Lauren! What is it?" you call as you race to catch up to her.

"The staircase is gone! Disappeared! We have no way to get back up above ground!" she shrieks.

"Hahahahaha!" The troll's laughter fills the cavernous room. "I've got you where I want you now, slaves! Trapped in the underworld of Woods-World!"

You turn your head right. Then left. You don't see the troll anywhere, but you know his power is there.

"Hurry, Lauren," you cry. "We have no choice. We have to go back through the tunnel to the cave. Maybe the power of the rose crystals is stronger than the troll's powers. Follow me!"

*Go to PAGE 58.*

"Okay, you little gnat," you snarl at the troll. "Your number is up!"

Using your new-found super strength, you pull a tree up by its roots. You swing it with the ease of a flyswatter. But just as the tree is about to swat the troll, he magically disappears.

"Ahahahahahahahahahahaha!" roars the pint-sized pest. He is now standing behind you. His laughter is even more annoying than the howl of the werewolves. And his whistle is more powerful than any muscles.

*"Tweeeeeeeeeeeeee!"* the troll's piercing whistle vibrates inside your ear. You return to your original skinny body. Your mega-muscles disappear. You quickly drop the tree. You are now powerless to resist the troll's orders.

"I am the Master of the Box, and I command you to go back to your cabin!" the troll says. Then he whistles again.

You head back to Evergreen Cabin. Todd and Lauren watch in disbelief. You're in a trance!

"Don't leave us!" Todd cries after you.

*Go to PAGE 72.*

"AAAAAAAAHHHHHHHHHH!" you and Todd scream together when you spot the drooling werewolves.

You start to run. You turn around to make sure Todd is keeping up with you. He's gone!

And the werewolf that was right on your heels is gone, too.

You race toward the dark end of the tunnel. The air gets thinner. It is hard to breathe. Soon you're light-headed from the lack of oxygen.

You feel as if you're floating. Is it true? Are you really floating?

*Go to PAGE 65.*

# 58

You grab Lauren's hand and start to run for the tunnel. Then you stop. You whirl around, confused. "Hey, where did the tunnel go?" you cry. "Which way do we go?"

"Is it this way?" the troll taunts. He magically appears to the left of you. "Or this way?" he says, popping up to the right of you. "Or this way? Or this way? Or this way?"

There's no way to tell which is the right way now. The cellar walls have turned into mirrors. They reflect off of each other. No matter what direction you turn, hundreds of reflections of the troll stare back at you.

"There are too many of them!" Lauren cries. "We can't escape!"

You spot a bucket of golf balls in the corner of the community center cellar. You grab a handful and start throwing the balls at each image. *CRASH!* One mirror image shatters. *CRASH!* Another troll reflection is smashed.

You continue throwing golf balls until there are only two reflections left — one in front of you and one behind you. You have only one ball left to throw. You must hit the real troll this time to escape.

---

*If you throw the ball at the troll in front of you, go to PAGE 101.*

*If you throw the ball at the troll behind you, go to PAGE 96.*

Before you can bring your foot down on the ants, Lauren pulls you back. "I think they're talking to us," she says. "In sign language! My best friend is deaf. She taught me how to sign."

"Talking ants?" Todd exclaims. "Now I've heard everything!"

"And I haven't heard anything — at least not from these ants," you say. You don't believe Lauren. Your legs are burning from their bites and stings. You start to bring your foot down on the ants again.

Lauren watches the ants carefully. "They say they're sorry they attacked us." She interprets their motions for you and Todd. "They say they were just scared."

"What else are they saying?" Todd asks.

"They say thank you for the magic O's," Lauren continues. "It was the magic O's that made them smart enough to communicate with us. They warn us to hold onto the magic O's. And use them only for emergencies."

Lauren watches some more, and a look of amazement comes over her face.

"What is it, Lauren?" you ask, one foot still in the air.

*Turn to PAGE 123.*

You feel yourself being drawn toward the community center. This is the building where guests at WoodsWorld meet to play cards, use the library, socialize, and eat at the snack bar or cafeteria.

You hear laughter and voices inside the community center building. Then you hear Mrs. Morris talking to your mom, "I just know this vacation is going to open Todd up to so many new experiences. He'll really grow from it!"

She can say that again! you think to yourself.

But you're not allowed to think to yourself. The troll is doing your thinking for you now. He is in your mind, controlling every move you make.

You tiptoe past the doorway to the big activity room where your parents, the Morrises, and Mr. and Mrs. Woods are all playing cards. Seeing them suddenly makes you want to run and tell them all about your troll troubles. Do you dare?

*Turn to PAGE 125.*

Oooops! You missed!

"Sorry, Todd," you call down into the bottomless pit. You lean over and watch Todd get smaller and smaller and smaller.

· You hear Todd's voice calling your name as he falls down, down, down, down, down, down, down, down, down, down, down, down,
down, down,
down, down. . . .

But you don't feel too bad. After all, it's a bottomless pit, so you know Todd will never ever reach

**THE END**

"Todd's right," you say for the first time. "This tree trunk is a big red fire ant colony!" You flip the switch on your flashlight. The light reveals thousands of angry ants marching on their enemies — you, Todd, and Lauren!

"These things will eat us alive!" Todd shouts. "I did a science report about them once."

"Shouldn't we get out of here?" Lauren asks. She slaps at a column of ants crawling up her bare legs. Their bites and stings make Lauren's legs puff up immediately. She can't get the red ants off her body. The ants keep stinging as they march toward her neck and face.

"Should we go back and face the werewolf?" Todd asks you.

"Or should we stay here and get eaten alive by these fire ants?" Lauren asks.

It's all up to you. You decide.

*If you turn back and risk meeting the werewolf, go to PAGE 18.*

*If you battle the army of ants, turn to PAGE 35.*

You ate the *O*'s from your right pocket. What does that mean? you wonder.

"These SUPER-STRENGTH O's aren't working at all!" Todd whines. "I feel even weaker than I did before I ate them."

"And you look really funny, Todd," Lauren says strangely.

"Aw, come on, Lauren," you start to defend your nerdy friend. "He can't help what he looks like."

*Wow, didn't YOU get nice suddenly! You had better sit down a minute and rest before you go on to PAGE 127.*

"Todd! Lauren! Sharky! Anybody! Help!" you cry. Calling for help is the only way you're going to escape the trolls.

"We're right here!" a voice answers you.

It's Todd's voice, but it's coming out of the mouth of the troll standing right on your knee.

"Yes, we're all here!" That's Lauren's voice coming out of the mouth of a different troll.

"Hey, dude, what's happening?" another troll says in Sharky's voice.

*What is happening?* you wonder.

"We were all turned into trolls," Todd explains. "And you're going to turn into a troll, too, and be our leader!"

"Me?" you shriek. "I'm going to turn into a creepy-looking, disgusting, tiny troll?"

"Your wish is my command, Master," says one of the trolls. He whistles shrilly and turns you into what you've just described. You're a troll!

What will the kids at school think when they see you?

"Oh, well," you say, "at least now that I'm so short I'll stand at the beginning of the lunch line instead of at

**THE END."**

Yes! You are floating!

Out of the cave. Into the darkness of the night.

You look down and see the lake far below. "Hello down there!" you call to anyone who might be awake in the cabins of WoodsWorld. No one hears you. No one sees you drifting, drifting awaaaaaaaay.

As you drift high above WoodsWorld your body starts to shrink. Suddenly you feel very light.

"Paper thin, that's what I am now," you say. "It must have been from not having enough oxygen and breathing that bad cave air."

You continue to shrink as you float toward the entrance to WoodsWorld. You see the main building. You see the cars parked around it. You see the string of brightly colored paper lanterns lit up to welcome newcomers to WoodsWorld.

You seem to be floating closer and closer to the lanterns. You've only seen them from the ground. This is the first time you're looking at them from above. It's the closest you've ever been to the paper lanterns.

"Oh, my!" you gasp when you notice the strangest thing you've seen all night.

*Hurry to PAGE 90.*

You notice that the ugly troll's commands have no effect on you. It doesn't take a genius to figure out the reason you've escaped his control. Your hands are still covering your ears! You can't hear the whistle that seems to have put Todd and Lauren into some kind of a trance. Without the vibrations of his whistle in your ears, your power to resist the troll is still strong.

Aha! you think. So he doesn't have *all* the power after all!

Whoops. You shouldn't have even thought that. The troll read your mind. And to prove you wrong, he says a troll word that sounds like *Gyzacck!*

You have no idea what that means, but you do know one thing — it's time to grab Lauren and Todd and get out of here.

"Run!" you shout into their faces. Their trance-like stares are broken at the sound of your voice. "Run!" you yell again.

*Race to PAGE 54.*

You're floating in a new tunnel now. You're sure of that. The feeling here is completely different. The tight grip of the waves in the Tunnel of Waves has loosened. You are floating on the surface of a calm, smooth body of water. The closeness of the tunnel's walls has given way to open air. Your eyes see nothing but blackness as you bob slowly up and down in the water. The sulfur smell is gone, replaced now by odorless air.

"I can breathe again!" you shout into the darkness.

"I can breathe again!" your own voice echoes back. "I can breathe again! I can breathe again!"

"Hello!" you cry, testing the echo again.

"Hello! Hello! Hello! Hello!" your voice returns from the pitch-black nothingness all around you.

You are alone. The only sound is the sound of your own voice. And the sound of your own breathing. . . . But wait! What's that other sound right next to your ear?

*Strain your ears to hear better on PAGE 23.*

"The werewolves!" Todd shouts. "Start howling!"

You grab Todd's shoulders and give him a good shake. "Snap out of it, Todd!" you order him.

"It's either howl or run," he insists. "And we don't know which way the werewolves are heading."

"There is one more choice, Todd," you reply. You point to a stream of light at the end of yet another tunnel. It looks as if it might be the way out. "There," you say.

"Oh, yeah, sure," Todd says nervously. "I already saw that tunnel. I also saw that giant hole in the floor between us and the way out. Just listen to this." Todd drops a loose stone into the hole. The two of you wait to hear it hit bottom.

It never does.

"A bottomless pit," Todd announces.

*HOW-OW-OW-OW-OWL!* This time the howling isn't coming from Todd. He's too busy talking about the pit.

"It's the werewolves," Todd whispers. "Start howling!"

"No, jump!" you shout.

---

*If you howl to save yourself, turn to PAGE 33.*
*If you jump across the bottomless pit, leap to PAGE 111.*

You decide to take the stairs to who-knows-where. You take a few steps down.

The good news about your new muscles is that they make you feel very powerful. The bad news is, they make you feel very stuck in this narrow staircase!

Your huge shoulders wedge between the two stone walls of the stairway. You head down, down, down, into a cellar you never knew existed. You hear voices coming from somewhere even further down.

"That troll is in complete control. We have no choice but to destroy everything in his power," Todd tells Lauren. "Friend or no friend, we have to save WoodsWorld."

What? you think. My own friends want to destroy me?

You've got to get out of here and prove that you are not working for the troll anymore. But how?

If you go back upstairs and break through the wall, go to PAGE 128.

If you hurry to the bottom of the stairs to face Lauren and Todd, race to PAGE 107.

". . . three!" you shout. You spring forward.

"We did it!" Todd says. He moves out of the way and watches you.

"What is this 'we' business?" you ask. You struggle alone to tie the sweatshirt around the werewolf's eyes.

*It is a well-known fact that if an animal's eyes are covered, it will not resist capture.* You have no idea where that information came from. It just popped into your brain. But you know that you know *everything* now.

Todd suddenly decides to help. He reaches for one end of the sweatshirt. By mistake he grabs the hair on the back of the werewolf's neck.

The werewolf roars in pain. It fights and struggles to escape. It turns in Lauren's direction. Her eyes are still covered with her hands, so she doesn't know what's about to happen. Even you and your smart mind can't stop the werewolf. It's going right for Lauren's face!

*Turn to PAGE 129.*

The full moon, the black sky, and the thought of werewolves in the woods help you decide what to do. You are definitely going back to the cabin. You can always hunt for the box in the morning.

As you walk along the path back to Evergreen Cabin, Lauren catches up with you. "I'm sure glad you're back this summer. This werewolf thing is really bad for business!"

"You don't really believe there are werewolves in these woods, do you, Lauren?" you ask.

"I didn't until I started hearing the howling," she says quietly. "Have you heard it yet?"

"Give me a break!" You laugh as you reach your cabin. "It's probably just the wind blowing through the trees."

"Yeah, probably," Lauren agrees. She nervously twists a strand of her long black hair around her finger. "Well, see you tomorrow."

The lights are all out in your cabin. You enter quietly. You tiptoe past your parents' and the Morrises' rooms. They're all sleeping. But you hear a noise coming from the room you are sharing with Todd. What is it?

*Go to PAGE 99.*

"Don't leave us," the troll imitates Todd's cries. "Hahahahahahahahaha! Your friend is useless to you now," he taunts Todd. "Useless! Hahahaha-hahahahaha!"

With his magic, the troll makes himself smaller. Then bigger. Then even smaller. He jumps from rock to rock changing his size with each jump. One minute he is the size of a gorilla. The next minute he's the size of a rat.

"Come back!" Todd shouts to you. "Please, come back!"

Are you strong enough to resist the troll's trance?

*If you can do five push-ups, go to PAGE 26.*
*If you can't do five push-ups, go to PAGE 120.*

You drop the library door and run. You leave the community center and head for the woods. Like a muscle-bound gorilla tearing through the jungle, you use your super-strength to push back the thin wall of bushes and trees that block your path.

You think you hear footsteps behind you. You slow down and turn around to look. But you see nothing and no one.

"How dare you run away!" the troll's voice sounds in your mind. "You must obey me at all times!"

While the troll gives you mental messages, the woods start moving all around you. At first it seems as if the trees are moving. But then you see them.

Trolls! The trolls are coming out of hiding.

Hundreds of the ugly little creatures are crawling through the woods. They are devouring leaves and sticks and dirt like maggots on rotten meat. They stuff their blubbery-lipped mouths full of anything they pick up. You feel sick as you watch the trolls chew with their mouths open and their thick tongues hanging out.

*Go to PAGE 40.*

There is a secret room on the other side of the wall. In the room you can't hear the troll's controlling whistle anymore. You feel your incredible strength returning.

You flex your muscles just to test them out. You wait until it seems safe, then you decide to push the bookshelf back.

Using one shoulder, you give the wall a shove.

It doesn't move. You push and shove with all your might. Nothing. Too bad. It looks as if the revolving bookcase locked behind you. Well, you do have these super-duper muscles — you could break down the wall. Or you could go down that stone staircase that you've just spied in the corner of this secret room. Hmmmmm . . . interesting choice.

*Break the wall? Crash through to PAGE 128.*
*Take the stairs to who-knows-where? Go to PAGE 69.*

"This way," you answer. "Toward the two red lights." You lead the way through a wall of thorny bushes. "There should be a path to the beach around here somewhere," you say.

"Youch!" Todd cries. "These stupid thorns are scratching me all up."

"Better watch out you don't bleed too much," you joke. "You don't want those werewolves to catch the scent of fresh blood!"

Todd's knees tremble as the two of you push through the overgrown vines and shrubs.

"Are you sure this is the path?" Todd asks. "It's so dark out here. I can't see a thing!"

Before you can answer, you hear *HOW-OW-OW-OWL!* This time the terrifying noise is very, very close.

"Oh, no!" Todd whines.

What *was* that sound? You try not to panic — for Todd's sake. You flip on the flashlight switch. Darkness still surrounds you. You hit the flashlight on your hand. Once, twice. Still no light.

"Stupid batteries," you mumble. But even without light, you notice the ground under your feet changing from dry to slippery and very slimy. Where are you?

*Go to PAGE 4.*

You have no power over your own actions. The choice has been made for you. You are going to search the cabins of WoodsWorld. The troll orders you to start your search with the cabin that is farthest away. You follow the path to a small log cabin deep in the woods. There is a sign hanging on a post in front of the cabin. It reads DOCTOR W. WOLFF.

Before you can sneak up to the door, it opens.

*Go to PAGE 44.*

The three of you stare down the dark tunnel. The darkness goes on forever. The decision is made instantly. "The stairs!" you all say at once.

You lead the way up the stairs. Todd is right behind you, and Lauren is behind him. You are careful, trying not to slip on the steep stairs. You look straight ahead and move very slowly. Before you get to the last step, you turn to make sure Todd and Lauren are still behind you.

It's so dark. You can't see anything.

"Lauren?" you call out. "Todd? Are you guys there?"

*If they are behind you, turn to PAGE 118.*
*If they are not behind you, go to PAGE 82.*

"Sharky was wrong when he said no one is safe here," you tell Todd. "I know what we have to do. There is one way to keep ourselves safe. The werewolf moon has no power over us as long as we stay out of its light!"

"You mean the light of the full moon is what started turning me into a werewolf?" Todd asks curiously.

"Exactly," you reply. "And if we stay out of the moonlight we'll be safe from werewolves. Do you get it?"

A low growl answers.

"Todd? Was that you?" you whisper.

*Hurry! Turn to PAGE 22, before it is too late!*

The super-strength trio run up the stairs and burst through the bookshelf wall of the library. You expect to come face to face with the enemy. But instead of one whistling troll, the three of you are greeted by *hundreds* of them.

"They've taken over the community center!" Lauren says. She uses her hands to talk in sign language.

"We're safe as long as our ears are plugged," you sign back.

The lead troll goes wild! "What's this?" he cries. "They're talking without talking! I can't hear them! And they can't hear us! Louder, you stupid tribe of trolls! Louder!"

He runs wildly through the crowd of trolls, shouting at them.

"Stand your ground!" you sign to the others. "He's going crazy because he can't control us."

Now many of the trolls are covering their ears to block out the deafening sounds of their own whistling.

"Louder! Louder! Louder, you fools!" the most wart-covered troll of all shouts.

---

*Hold your ears on PAGE 108.*

"You caught me!" Todd exclaims, grabbing your hand.

"We caught each other!" you sputter. Your hands grasp Todd's hands over the center of the hole. "Oh, no! We're f-a-a-a-a-a-a-l-l-i-n-g!"

"I can't look!" Todd shrieks.

"Oh, brother," you think, as you feel your arms and legs become all tangled up with Todd's. "Just my luck. Of all the people in the world I could have fallen into a bottomless pit with, it has to be Todd Morris!"

Down, down, down you fall.

Spinning and tumbling head over heels over head over heels with no end in sight.

Todd sticks to you like syrup to pancakes. And now that you think of it — he's probably getting that syrupy slug juice all over you, too! You're not sure which is worse — having Todd glued to you or being slimed by slugs.

You have plenty of time to think about it, since you'll be free-falling for quite a while!

*Fall over to PAGE 38.*

"Come on, Todd," you say. You reach over and hold onto his arm. "We're going in the cave. We're not going to let those Murphy brothers scare us, are we?"

"We aren't?" gulps Todd. "I mean, no! We aren't!"

A thin beam of moonlight shines into the mouth of the cave. You can see that the floor is pure slime.

You take one step forward. Your feet fly up into the air. You land flat on your back and bring Todd down with you.

Then you and Todd start sliding faster and faster.

"WHOA-A-A-A-A-A-A-A!" Your two voices blend into one. You squeeze your eyes shut. You feel as if you are sliding down the world's steepest water slide.

Down, down you go. Faster. Faster. You and Todd zoom down a slime-slicked tunnel in total darkness.

Just when you think your body can't take one more second of this wild ride, it ends with a grand-slam *BAM*! You smash into a wet cave wall.

---

*If you open your eyes now, go to PAGE 85.*

*If you can't bear to look, keep your eyes closed and try to turn to PAGE 7.*

Todd and Lauren are not behind you!

You turn around and start to go back down the stairs to see what happened to them. *BLAM!* Something soft hits you in the face. It feels like a large pillow. You can't breathe. You scream as loud as you can.

"What's all the screaming in here?" you hear your dad ask.

You pull the big pillow off your face. You see your dad gazing down at you.

"Time to get up," he says. "Come on. Todd's waiting for you to go to the kids-only campfire. You must have dozed off for a few minutes while you were unpacking."

"Kids-only campfire?" you ask in a daze. "Haven't we already done that?"

"Every year, the same old same old," your dad mutters. "Just like always. Nothing unexpected ever happens at WoodsWorld. You can always count on that."

"Whatever you say, Dad." You smile. "Whatever you say."

You learned a long time ago that saying "whatever you say, Dad" is the perfect reply when you want to bring a conversation with your dad to

**THE END**

The scene in the snack bar room is straight out of one of those late-night science fiction movies. All the guests of WoodsWorld, including Lauren and Todd, are sitting at tables eating heaping bowls of SUPER-STRENGTH O's. As they eat, they stare straight ahead. Before you enter the room, you put on the Walkman earphones. You hope they'll protect you from the troll's whistle. No one even notices you. Well, no one except the troll.

The wicked little man is standing on a high stool behind the snack bar. His blubbery lips slobber drool down his wart-covered chin as he dishes out the food to a line of guests. Between spoonfuls, he takes time out to whistle the piercing whistle. This keeps his slaves totally in his control. They are weak until he decides he needs their super-strength powers to carry out his orders.

You get on the food line. You plan to knock the troll off the stool when you reach the front of the line. The guests move in a trance toward their helping of O's. The troll puckers up his lips and is about to whistle again. Will the earphones keep you safe?

*Go to PAGE 115.*

Well, of course you're too nice to throw anyone to the wolves — even the Murphys. But while you give the idea a moment of serious thought, something very strange happens.

Instead of clawing and biting and tearing at the bodies of the three Murphy bullies, the wolves hug them. They even kiss them! They pat them on the back and give big, fanged smiles to all three brothers!

The werewolves are treating the Murphys like family!

"Look at that!" you say to Todd. "The Murphys are so mean because it runs in the family — the werewolf family!

"That explains why the Murphys smell just like a pack of dirty, hairy, scary werewolves," you continue with a laugh. "A simple case of Wolfatosis!"

Todd laughs at your jokes, but there's nothing funny about having the werewolves' hot breath blowing right in your face. You'd better start running, or for you and Todd it's sure to be

**THE END**

You and Todd hit the cave wall with a giant *THUD*.

You both open your eyes at the same time and see the same eerie sight.

Eyes! Hundreds, no thousands, of bright yellow eyes. Eyes on the ceiling, on the walls, on the floor.

"Bats!" Todd exclaims. He sounds more amazed than scared. "They won't hurt us. I studied all about them for a science report."

You're not so sure Todd's right. Two bats fly right by your face. Their yellow eyes whiz past you like shooting stars. The flapping of their webbed wings creates a breeze that sends chills down your spine.

You whip your head around to move out of the bats' flight path. As you duck down, you feel bat wings brush across your face. Their tiny claws catch in your hair. Then they fly away, yanking out small clumps of your hair as they go.

The bats surround you. You turn to find Todd. It's hard to see through the thousands of flapping black wings. Where is he?

*Go to PAGE 42.*

With a heave and a ho, the band of trolls hurls the whistling leader far into Deep Woods Lake. The cold lake water slowly sucks him down. With a giant *BLURRRP*, the lake swallows the troll forever.

The crowd of trolls lining the shore of the lake cheers. They seem a little less gruesome now that their wicked leader is gone. You glance over at Todd and Lauren and notice that their muscles are gone, too. So are yours.

The three of you have your normal shapes back. You all take out your ear plugs. Together you throw your fists up in the air and shout, "We have the power!"

And from down at the south end of the beach you hear the Murphy brothers shouting, "Way to go, Nerdo!" They are holding out Todd's red tin box.

"Here's your box back, Nerdo," Sharky calls. "You deserve it."

Todd just smiles that goofy-looking smile and says, "I think they like me better now, don't you?"

You don't know how the Murphys feel. But in your opinion, Todd "Nerdo" Morris is one cool dude. And you're going to hate having this vacation come to

**THE END**

"Sorry, Sharky," you say.

"You have to help us," Sharky calls out, when he spots you and Todd. "We didn't mean any harm."

Now the werewolves see you. You have to think fast.

"Tell me where the box is, and I'll save all of you," you shout above the growls and snarls.

"The werewolves have it!" Buck Murphy cries out. "That's why we came in here!"

"Yeah, we were trying to get it back for your friend, or whatever he is," Jess explains.

You watch in horror as the werewolves lick their chops. Rows of sharpened fangs glisten in the glow of the werewolves' red eyes. They are ready for the Murphy feast.

"Please," Sharky begs. "Help us. Please!"

*Go to PAGE 27.*

You and Todd agree you've had enough of the werewolves. "Let's keep going down," you say.

"Yes," Todd agrees. "This pterodactyl has figured out how to stay alive for centuries. Maybe it will know how to keep us alive for the rest of the night!"

"Good thinking," you reply. Then to the pterodactyl, you order, "Down please!"

With a giant flapping of his bony wings, the prehistoric creature points its head downwards. You and Todd hold on to the loose flaps of skin on its neck.

Down, down, down the pterodactyl flies.

Without warning, the downward flight takes a turn to the left. You shine the flashlight straight ahead and spot a ledge.

Todd sees it, too. "Look!" he shouts, pointing to the ledge. "We're going to land over there!"

*Go to PAGE 98.*

"What is it, Lauren?" you and Todd exclaim. You both reach her at the same time.

"I went the wrong way! I saw the troll! So I turned down another tunnel and ended up on the other side of the Cave of Rose Crystals," Lauren explains. "I walked through the cave, and here I am back at this tunnel!"

"What!?" Todd shouts in his nerdy way. "We all discovered the greatest treasure in the world together. Are you saying you went *in* the treasure cave without us?"

Lauren can't stop laughing.

"What's so funny?" you ask.

"The Cave of the Rose Crystals," Lauren says. "It isn't the greatest treasure in the world. It is a storeroom for the souvenirs of WoodsWorld! These aren't rose crystals — they're plastic!"

"You mean it's not a treasure?" Todd asks.

"Not unless you like pink plastic heart necklaces that say 'My heart belongs to WoodsWorld.'" Lauren giggles.

"All our hearts do belong to WoodsWorld. It's where we always go every summer," you say. "That's why we have to save it from the troll!" You look into the dark tunnel and wonder what to do.

*Turn to PAGE 77.*

You are floating directly above the paper lanterns now. For the first time, you see that each lantern has a face!

In fact, each lantern has a face of someone you have known in the past. Hanging on the line of lanterns are all the people who used to come to WoodsWorld. For reasons you never understood before, they just stopped coming in the summers!

But now you know the truth. They didn't stop coming to WoodsWorld. They never left!

Slowly you drift up and over to an empty space on the string of colored paper lanterns. You hear a soft click. Suddenly you can't move.

"Hey!" you try to say to someone, anyone. But you're a paper-lantern person now. You can't talk anymore. And neither can any of the other lantern people.

Hope you like WoodsWorld a lot. You'll be hanging around here for a long, long time. In fact your stay here may never, ever come to an

**END**

"Oomphh!" the werewolf puffs as you pounce on it.

"Sorry," you say. "I have to help the Murphys." You use all your strength to pull the werewolf off the Murphys. You can't do it alone. "Help me, Todd!" you plead.

Todd looks at the Murphys and at you. Then he stares at the werewolf who was his friend, if only for a few minutes. Todd knows what he has to do. He jumps on the werewolf with you. Together you knock it to the ground.

"The Murphys do deserve to cry," Todd says as he struggles with the beast. "But they don't deserve to be a three-course meal for a werewolf."

"Grrrrrrr . . . GRRRRRRRRRR . . ." roars the werewolf. It twists back and forth with new strength. You and Todd have freed the Murphys. Now the werewolf runs free, too. He runs into the darkness with an ear-piercing *HOW-OW-OW-OW-OWL*. Even though you and Todd tried your hardest, the werewolf has escaped.

You're exhausted. You, Todd, Lauren, and the Murphys fall on the ground. The last thing you remember is staring up at the dark sky. A full moon stares back.

*Go to PAGE 34.*

You ate the *O*'s out of your left pocket. And the left pocket was the right pocket!

"I feel like Superman!" Todd cries. His arm muscles stretch his T-shirt sleeves to the breaking point.

"How about Superperson," Lauren corrects Todd. "We all have equal super-strength now."

The three of you raise clenched fists in the air and shout, "We have the power!"

But Todd can't just leave it at that. He's got to go on and on with the corny stuff. "We are the super-strong trio! We promise to fight for truth, power, and justice for all —"

A soft *"tweeeeeeet"* interrupts Todd's declaration.

"It's the troll!" Lauren cries. "He's going to take away our power again!"

"Not if we can help it, he won't," you reply. You begin tearing off pieces of your shirt sleeves and stuffing them into your ears. "If we can't hear him, he can't hurt us," you remind the others.

Lauren and Todd plug up their ears, too — and not a minute too soon. The troll's piercing whistle is shaking the whole staircase, but the three of you don't hear a thing.

*Go to PAGE 79.*

"Todd!" you exclaim when you hear his voice right next to you. "What's happening? How did I catch up to you so fast?"

"You didn't." Todd laughs. "We caught up to you!"

Before Todd can say more, you realize that you are no longer falling. You and Todd are both sitting on the back of some giant-winged thing.

"What the . . . ?" you start to ask.

"It's a pterodactyl!" Todd explains. "Probably preserved in this pit for centuries!"

The huge, prehistoric flying reptile is moving its head — first up, then down. It seems to be asking you to choose which way you want to go — up or down?

*To fly up to the werewolves, soar to PAGE 116.*
*To go down to the unknown, zoom to PAGE 88.*

Yes, you definitely need time to think of a way out of this mess you're in now. You're flat on your back in the land of the little people. You're tied to the ground and covered from head to toe with disgusting, ugly trolls.

They take turns examining you. Slobbering, glop-dropping trolls peer down your throat, up your nose, and under your eyelids.

The trolls may be little, but their breath is big, bad, and ugly! You decide you've had enough.

It's time for your secret plan.

*For the secret plan, go to PAGE 104.*

"Have no fear, super-strength is here!" you call out. Lauren and Todd are still screaming. The werewolf moves closer and closer to them.

Using your ordinary strength, you open the box. You expect to see some mega-vitamins. Instead the box is filled with very ordinary-looking oat *O*'s cereal.

The werewolf snarls. Then it lunges right for Todd's throat.

"Save us!" Todd shouts.

"Here goes," you say. You toss a fistful of *O*'s into your mouth. The effect is instant. Super-strength fills your body. Your shirt rips at the seams. Enormous muscles bulge and burst out of the torn material.

"Wow!" you gasp. "This could be fun!"

But you know that looks aren't everything. Are these new muscles as strong as they appear to be?

The werewolf is ready to dig its fangs into Todd's neck. You flex your muscles. Another seam tears open at the shoulder of your shirt. You place a finger under the werewolf's arm and start to lift.

"Oh, no. I hope this works," you pray.

*Turn to PAGE 17.*

You take aim at the troll behind you. You hurl the golf ball directly at the center of his forehead.

"Arrrrrgh!" the troll roars in agony. "You got me!"

Then the strange little creature begins to shrivel and shrink right before your eyes.

"Agony! Agony!" he cries, holding his head. He's growing smaller and smaller. Slowly, the troll disappears.

All that is left of him is a small pile of SUPER-STRENGTH O's cereal!

"He's gone!" Lauren exclaims.

"And so are we," you say to her. "Let's get Todd and get out of here. Go on ahead. I want to get something."

Reluctantly, Lauren runs down the tunnel alone. You bend down and pick up the pile of O's that used to be the troll. As you put them in your pocket, you hear a familiar wicked laugh in your mind. It is the laugh of the troll.

Uh-oh, you think. The troll isn't gone!

Then Lauren screams.

*Go to PAGE 89.*

"Well, look who's here. Nerdo and his pals." Sharky Murphy sneers. "Still looking for that box of yours?" Sharky and his brothers push their way through the bushes.

"Hey, what's that other box over there?" Jess asks. He points to the rocking box, which is now bumping around even more.

"Nothing to worry about," you say as you reach into your pockets and pull out some SUPER-STRENGTH O's. "You boys hungry?"

Todd's looking at you like you're totally crazy!

"Care for a little midnight snack?" you offer nicely.

"Give me all of it!" Sharky snaps. He grabs the handout. "Here," he says, passing some O's to Buck and Jess. "It's free!"

As the Murphys chomp on the O's, the box jumps up and down. "No! No!" the troll shouts from inside the box.

Sharky leans down to pick up the jumping box. He puts his ear to it to listen. "What the . . . ?" he starts to say, but a sudden growth spurt of gigantic muscles stops him.

*Jump to PAGE 36.*

The pterodactyl nose-dives down to the ledge with a great swooping motion. You and Todd are sure you're going to be thrown over the creature's head. But the pterodactyl evens out its flight and glides to a smooth landing. The two of you tumble off its back and onto the rocky ground.

"Thank —" you start to say. Before you can get the whole word out, its wings are flapping again. The pterodactyl is heading back into the darkness of the pit. You and Todd are left alone on the narrow ledge.

Behind you there's a door! It slides open.

"Going down?" a man dressed in an elevator operator's uniform asks.

"Do we have a choice?" Todd asks.

"Always," the man says mysteriously.

*Go to PAGE 117.*

The noise you hear is Todd crying into his pillow. You are too tired to talk now. Instead, you kick off your sneakers and climb into your bed with your clothes on. Just as you start to drift off to sleep, you hear *HOW-OW-OW-OW-OWL!*

"Did you hear that?" Todd cries. He jumps out of bed and hurries over to your bedside. The light from the full moon casts an eerie glow over Todd's terrified face.

"Don't be afraid. It's only the wind howling," you mutter.

*HOW-OW-OW-OWL!*

Todd leaps onto your bed and screams, "It's a wild animal!"

Before you can answer, a rock with a note attached flies through your open window and lands on the wooden floor. You push Todd aside and wriggle out of bed. You pick the rock up, tear the note off, and read aloud:

"The Werewolves of WoodsWorld
They love to see red,
So the box that was yours
Is now their box instead!
The Werewolves of WoodsWorld
Disappear at dawn,
So you must find the box
Before this night is gone!"

---

*Turn to PAGE 8.*

You crawl into the dark tunnel. Todd and Lauren follow close behind. You only have to crawl a short distance before the tunnel gets larger. You stand up straight and see a rose-colored glow ahead. It's magically pulling you toward it.

"What is it?" Lauren asks. Her face looks pink in the glow of the light.

"The Cave of the Rose Crystals!" Todd exclaims. "Geologists have been searching for this cave for years. The crystals are supposed to have magic powers."

"What kinds of powers?" you ask.

"No one really knows for sure," Todd explains. "But I read in a book that the last explorers to go into the caves never came out."

"Then why are we going in?" Lauren asks. "I'm not crazy. I'm turning back!"

Lauren turns and runs out of the cave. Seconds later you hear her scream.

---

QUICK! If you tell Todd to wait there while you investigate Lauren's screams, turn to PAGE 55.

Or let the power of the Rose Crystals pull you to PAGE 89.

You pull your arm back over your head and let the golf ball fly at the troll in front of you. *CRASH!* Another mirror shatters.

"Hahahahahahahaha!" laughs the troll behind you. "Wrong choice, losers!"

You and Lauren spin around to face the real troll. Behind him there is a mirror in which you see your own reflections. The troll has won.

But something is strange. Really strange.

You stare into the mirror again. Lauren no longer looks like Lauren. And you no longer look like you!

"We look like Todd!" Lauren exclaims. "He turned us into Todds!"

Nerd Alert! Nerd Alert!

Your second worst nerdmare has just come true. Now you're not just spending your vacation with a nerd. You'll be spending the rest of your life *as* a nerd.

You open your mouth to speak and can't believe what comes out. In Todd's voice you say, "Hey, hey! What do you say! This looks like a swell way to come to

**THE END."**

"Aaaaaaahhhhhhhhh!" you hear from the darkness below you. It's Todd, and he sounds very far away. You have lost him now for sure.

Too bad, you think sadly. I was just starting to get used to having him around.

"Good-bye, Todd," you call as loudly as you can. "I'm sorry I said you were a nerd. I really do like you, you know. Honest!" With tears in your eyes, you call out one last " 'Bye, Todd. I'll miss you . . . really, I will!"

"You really will miss me?" a happy voice calls out unexpectedly, right next to your ear. "Wow! That's swell!"

*Huh? What's going on here? Turn to PAGE 93.*

Your mind is racing. In seconds, every math fact you ever learned pops into your head. Every spelling word you ever studied flashes before you. The theory of relativity, the Gettysburg Address, a map of Marco Polo's entire journey — you know it all. Every fact and every piece of trivia you've ever heard is right there in your mind. You've never felt so smart in your life.

"The *O*'s!" you exclaim. "The cereal in the SMARTS BOX is smart food!"

"Let's be smart, then," Lauren cries, peeking out from behind her hands. "Let's run while the werewolf is busy with the food!"

Immediately your brilliant brain has another idea.

"We're going to capture this werewolf and show it to the world," you announce.

"Don't be stupid!" Lauren shouts. "We have to run — now!"

*Think fast! What is it going to be?*
*If you try to capture the werewolf, turn to* PAGE 16.
*If you decide to run, race as fast as you can to* PAGE 45.

# 104

You have a secret plan you think just may work. "Hey, trolls!" you call out sweetly. "You forgot to examine my ears. Why don't you have a look?"

You can see they're curious. They talk in whispers for a few seconds. Then they creep close to your ears and peer in. Their noses fit right into your ear canals. That's just what you were hoping would happen. With the trolls' noses in your ears, you can't hear a thing.

Quickly, you use your tongue to remove a SUPER-STRENGTH O's food particle that's caught in between your teeth. You swallow the particle and feel the results immediately. Muscles!

The two trolls whose noses are plugging up your ears aren't paying attention to the muscles growing. But all the other trolls see it and begin to whistle.

With your muscles bulging and your shirt seams splitting again, you work fast to break through the ropes that hold you. When your hands are free, you press the two trolls against your ears. You use them like earmuffs to keep out the sounds of the whistling.

*Go to PAGE 39.*

It's no use. The werewolves cannot fight the sorceress's crystal light. One by one, with a *HOWL* as empty and hopeless as the Bottomless Pit itself, each werewolf loses its balance. They all fall backwards into the endless nothing that is the Pit.

Falling, falling, falling forever. Their howls rise to the open mouth of the Pit, filling the cave and the deep, dark woods surrounding WoodsWorld.

The Murphys throw themselves at you with heartfelt thanks for saving their lives. "We'll always remember you for this," Sharky says. "You too, Ner . . . I mean . . . hey, what is your name anyway?"

"This is my good friend, Todd Morris," you say. You put your arm around Todd's shoulder. You and Todd take the red tin box and lead the way out of the cave.

Nothing can frighten you or Todd now. Not the Murphys. Not the werewolves. You have faced every possible fear and conquered them all. For you both this should be a very happy

**END**

A candle burns in a jar next to a large boulder on the side of the path. As you hurry closer, a breeze makes the flame flicker. There's a note taped to the large rock.

You bend down and grab the note. Did someone leave this for *you*? You draw the candle close, squinting in the darkness to read the writing.

Wax drips, then hardens on the side of the jar, as you read the note aloud:

> "The Werewolves of WoodsWorld
> They love to see red,
> So the box that was Todd's
> Is now their box instead!
> The Werewolves of WoodsWorld
> Disappear at dawn,
> So you must find the box
> Before this night is gone!"

Werewolves? This must be a joke, you tell yourself. But you can't help gazing into the darkness. Searching. You hold your breath and listen.

Then you hear the crackling of twigs. Footsteps! You're not alone after all. Someone or something is out here with you!

*Go to PAGE 133.*

You creep quickly and quietly down the stairs. You notice your muscles getting smaller and smaller.

"We have to save WoodsWorld," Todd tells Lauren again. "But I sure don't know how."

"Maybe I can help," you say from the shadows. "Did you miss me?"

"You're free!" Lauren cries out when she sees you. "And your muscles are gone."

"It seems the farther underground I went, the smaller my muscles got. And as long as we can't hear the troll's whistle, we're safe," you explain.

"But how did you escape from him?" Lauren asks. "And how did you get down here? And how —"

"Hold on, hold on," you interrupt. "It's a long story. We don't have time to talk now. Right now we've got to get out of here and stop the troll before he takes over WoodsWorld and maybe even the whole world!"

"But how do we get out of here?" Todd asks.

"Well," you say, searching around the cellar for the best answer. "We can go up the stairs. Or we can go through that tunnel over there." You point across the cellar to a dark tunnel.

Which way will you go?

*Climb up the stairs on PAGE 77.*
*Go through the dark tunnel on PAGE 100.*

"Grab them!" the lead troll orders frantically. "Tackle them!"

Hundreds of tiny trolls leap through the air. They land on your arms, in your hair, on the back of your neck. With your super-strength, you easily fling the creatures aside. Lauren and Todd are having the same luck with the ones who have landed on them.

The battle rages on and on. But the SUPER-STRENGTH O's keep working. At last the trolls are defeated.

"Get up you lazy, toadstool mats!" the lead troll shouts to the other trolls. "I order you to fight for your troll leader. Me!" He scurries from place to place, kicking the other trolls, pulling their ears, yanking their fat, blubbery lips. "Fight! Fight! Fight!"

Then something changes. The trolls are no longer fighting you, Lauren, and Todd. Now they have turned against their leader. A crowd of angry trolls sweeps the leader off his feet. They lift him high above their ugly heads and carry him to the lake.

*Follow them to PAGE 86.*

The werewolves' frozen faces begin to move grotesquely. As they start to thaw, the werewolves open their jaws. Their fangs gleam in the full moon's light.

You watch the hairy, fanged beasts with fascination. They seem to communicate to one another in low growls and short howls. When all of them seem to be totally unfrozen, the leader of the pack leads the way out through the open ice door. The pack of wolves walk right past you. They don't notice you pressed flat against the wall.

You watch as they lumber into the cave. When the last one has passed, you wait a few seconds. Then you follow the sound of their low growls through the dark cave.

Where are they going?

*Follow the werewolves to PAGE 130.*

# 110

All three of you pick a different mound of fresh dirt and start digging with your hands. In minutes you and Lauren stand up at the exact same time and shout, "I found it!"

You both are holding up identical-looking red tin boxes.

"My collection!" Todd shrieks.

You take a closer look at the two boxes. "Sorry, Todd," you announce. "I don't think either one of these boxes is the one we're looking for."

Lauren hands you the box she found. You show Todd that one box is labeled SMARTS BOX. The other is labeled SUPER-STRENGTH BOX. You are just about to open them, when you hear a chilling *HOW-OW-OW-OW-OWL!*

A thunderous crashing noise comes from the woods in front of you. Something is coming toward you! Fear grips you. You clutch the two boxes tightly.

*HOW-OW-OW-OW-OWL!*

You dash across the path and crouch behind a large rock.

The wall of bushes bursts apart. A snarling, red-eyed, sharp-fanged beast bounds through the leaves.

"Aaaaaaaahhhhhhhhhhh!" Todd and Lauren scream.

*Go to PAGE 24.*

"We have to jump across the pit," you insist. "It may be the only way out of this place."

"I can't do it," Todd whines. "You'll have to go first."

As soon as you hear the howling again, all your nervousness disappears. "Come on, Todd!" you cry. "The werewolves are getting closer."

Without another word, you back up a few steps and take a running leap. It is so dark you can't be sure if you're making it across the pit or not. All you know is you're flying through the air.

In seconds your feet land on solid ground. Dirt crumbles under your heels. You are half on, half off the edge of the pit.

"Whoooooa!" you cry, swaying back and forth over the open pit.

"Don't leave me!" Todd screams.

"I'm trying my best not to," you snap. You fall forward onto the ground in front of you. "Whew! That was a close —"

You can't finish this sentence because what you see standing behind Todd is making your mouth drop wide open.

*Go to PAGE 41.*

In the light of the full moon you see the doctor's face. Long, coarse hair covers his forehead, cheeks, and chin. His eyes flash like a red fire. Fangs glisten as he opens his mouth — ready to bite.

Your screams fill the night air. But no one can hear you so far away. Behind you a gate comes crashing down around the cabin. There is no escape. The search for Todd's red tin box has brought you right to the werewolves of Woods-World. And also right to

## THE END

Air in. Air out. Air in. Air out.

With the next air in, your floating speeds up. You're no longer bobbing slowly up and down on a calm body of water. Now you are being towed by some force you cannot see.

"Help!" you scream.

"Help! Help!" your own voice echoes.

"Oh, it's no use," you cry.

"Oh, it's no use! Oh, it's no use!" the echo agrees with you.

In one final pull of the air force, you are sucked into another tunnel. A long narrow tunnel. You zoom through the tunnel and land in a dark pit. "Oh, no!" you sob.

But this time there is no echo.

There is only a loud *BURP*.

The Deep Woods Lake monster has just swallowed you whole! Sad to say, you're all washed up. For you, this story has come to . . .

**THE END**

# 114

The troll jumps out of the box and immediately makes himself bigger again. He begins to whistle and shout at the Murphy brothers. They try to cover their ears, but the muscles on their arms are too huge. They can't lift their own arms to their ears.

"Hahahahahahahaha," the troll laughs. "Now you are my slaves! You will obey me! Where is the red tin box the others are looking for? Tell me now!"

You, Todd, and Lauren watch in disbelief as the Murphys' muscles start shrinking. When the muscles are gone, the Murphys themselves start shrinking, too.

"Where is the box?" the troll repeats. "Tell me now, before I reduce you down to nothing!"

In a voice much smaller than his usual voice, Sharky calls out the answer the troll is looking for.

"What did he say?" Todd asks you. "Where is my box?"

*Go to PAGE 43.*

The troll watches you very closely. Someone behind you taps your shoulder and talks to you. You don't hear her because of the earphones. The troll watches as she talks to you again. Again you don't answer.

"What's the matter?" the troll asks right in your face so you can read his lips. "Troll got your tongue? Or are you just a little hard of hearing?" Then the wicked little creature reaches over with his clawlike fingers and yanks the earphones off your head.

His whistle fills your ears. You feel your muscles disappearing and all your own will going with them.

"You will sit when I sit," snarls the troll.

"Yes, Master," you say in a trance.

"You will promise to obey me always and forever," he growls at you.

"Yes, Master," you say weakly.

"You will be silent until I say your time to be silent has come to

**THE END."**

"Go up!" you command.

"I think I'm going to," Todd says in a queasy voice.

"I said *go* up, not *throw* up!" you yell.

The pterodactyl instantly points its head upward and flaps its wings hard. Up, up, up you rise. You soar through the darkness at speeds you never thought possible.

"Wow!" Todd exclaims. "This thing really moves!"

He's right. In fact, as you look up you realize the pterodactyl has moved so fast you're almost at the mouth of the Bottomless Pit. And you're also almost at the mouths of a pack of very hungry werewolves.

Their fang-filled mouths are watering!

*Fly to PAGE 15.*

You peer over the ledge and see a greater nothing than you've ever seen. You gaze up. Darkness. You glance down again. Darkness. Either way, it looks the same to you — totally frightening.

"I guess we'd better get in the elevator," you announce. You push Todd forward into the waiting car.

The door closes behind you and Todd.

A whirring sound begins, but you don't feel any motion. The closet-sized space is illuminated by a dim red light. The light seems to be blinking on, off, on, off, on, off. Then you figure it out!

The red light is on when the elevator operator's eyes are open and off when his eyes are closed. On when they're open. Off when they're closed. His *eyes* are the blinking red lights!

In the red glow, you notice the man's teeth are growing longer and sharper.

Todd elbows you sharply and cries, "He's one of them!"

*Go to PAGE 11.*

"We're here," Lauren says from the darkness.

"Keep up with me, guys," you instruct.

"I'm trying to," Lauren answers, "but I feel so weak."

"Me, too," Todd whines. "I have no strength."

"Well, fine superheroes you all turned out to be," you tease them. "How are we going to get rid of the troll if you can't even get up the stairs?"

You reach into your pocket and pull out a small fistful of SUPER-STRENGTH O's. "Here," you say, holding your hand out to your friends. "This should help. As long as we're underground the troll has no power. Get your strength back with these O's."

The three of you eat a little bit of the O's and sit on the stairs waiting for the expected results. You casually put your hand in your other pocket and pull out another handful of O's. They look exactly like the other O's, but you know you only had SUPER-STRENGTH O's in *one* pocket.

Uh-oh! Somebody must have planted other O's in the other pocket.

*If you ate from the right pocket, go to PAGE 63.*

*If you ate from the left pocket, go to PAGE 92.*

No scream comes out of your mouth. You quickly see the "horrible beasts" coming through the woods are none other than Sharky, Jess, and Buck Murphy!

"Did someone mention Murphys?" Sharky whoops. He runs right up to Todd and gives him a shove. "Well, Nerdo, here we are. Big as life and twice as scary!"

"So you haven't found your stupid box yet?" Jess taunts.

Buck sneaks up behind Todd and pinches his ear. In an evil-sounding voice he whispers, "Did the werewolves get you yet? Heh, heh."

Buck's laughter doesn't last long. It stops in his throat when a hairy hand pinches *his* ear. Then a growling voice whispers, "Did someone mention werewolves?"

It's Todd's werewolf friend! The SMARTS BOX food must have worn off. Todd's friend isn't so well-mannered anymore! All that is left is its ability to talk.

"It looks like I'm getting the last laugh," the werewolf growls at the trembling Murphy brothers.

*Go to PAGE 46.*

The troll's trance is too powerful. You've never felt so helpless, so weak, so weird!

"Go back to your cabin and await further instruction. I will be seeing you," the troll's hypnotic voice repeats in your mind. "Go back. Go back. Go back."

The troll controls your steps in the direction of the cabin. You climb onto the porch and open the door to Evergreen Cabin. Your parents and the Morrises are not home yet. No one has even noticed that you and Todd are not in bed.

In your mind you hear the troll's voice giving you all your instructions. You have no choice but to obey. You are in his power. You move mechanically to the bathroom to brush your teeth. You reach for the toothpaste. Instead your hand wraps around the leg of the troll!

*Go to PAGE 48.*

The werewolves have all lowered their arms and turned at once. They're licking their bloodthirsty lips. Their eyes glow like flaming torches.

One of the hairy beasts grabs Todd and breathes hot, stinking wolf breath in his face.

"No, please!" cries Todd. You can see tears gush from his wide eyes. "You can have the collection!" he tries to bargain.

The werewolf snarls and bares pointed fangs. Its mouth opens wide enough to take Todd's whole head in one bite.

"*HOW-OW-OW-OWL!*" you howl. You try to draw the werewolf's attention away from Todd.

It works! In fact the whole pack of werewolves turns away from the Murphys and Todd. All werewolf eyes are on you!

But you're ready for them.

In one swift motion you open the box and hold up the pewter sorceress. Their red eyes reflect off the crystal sun in the sorceress's hands. A blinding light is thrown back into the wolves' eyes. The wolves step backwards. They try to escape the reflecting light rays. Can they?

*Go to PAGE 105.*

# 122

You reach into your pocket and feel what you are looking for.

"Jawbreakers!" you announce to Lauren. You hold out a handful of round, colored candies. Then you toss them to the ground.

The pack of werewolves pounce on the jaw-breakers. They start chomping. In no time, pained howls fill the woods. *HOW-OW-OW-OWL-OWWWWWL!* All the hairy creatures cry out in jaw-breaking agony. Your plan worked.

"I knew my plan would work," you brag to Lauren. "Those fanged beasts won't be biting anyone for a long, long time."

Right again, genius. All the werewolves' teeth and fangs are broken and shattered. The jaw-breakers and your brilliant brain saved you and your friends. Now that you've cracked the case, you'll be free to keep searching and searching and searching for Todd's box until

**THE END**

Lauren has a very serious look on her face. She watches the motions of the red fire ants as they speak to her in sign language. "They say beware of the werewolves of WoodsWorld," she says. "They say we are not safe until we have the red tin box back in our hands."

"Do they know where it is?" Todd asks.

"They say they know, but they can't tell us. There's another power in the woods that we haven't seen yet," Lauren continues. "They say we must keep searching for the box — we only have until dawn to find it."

"That's right!" you exclaim. You take the folded note out of your pocket and read the poem again:

"The Werewolves of WoodsWorld
Disappear at dawn.
So you must find the box
Before this night is gone."

"There's no time to waste," you say to the others. "Lauren, tell the ants we're sorry we smashed into their tree. We won't hurt them if they don't hurt us. Our troubles are just beginning, but tell the ants their troubles with us have come to an

**END**

You throw open the red tin box and look at the pewter figure collection for the first time.

"Awesome!" you cry when you see the treasure. Inside the box are the most finely crafted, beautifully jeweled pewter figurines you've ever seen. "Yes," you say to Todd. "It was definitely worth the trouble."

Each figure is in its own velvet-lined compartment. You can't resist taking out the pewter dragon with the emerald eyes.

"Incredible," you whisper. You turn the figure around in your hand and study the details. You return the dragon to its compartment. One by one, you take out each figure and study it. There's a prince waving a crystal-bladed sword in the air, a ruby-studded castle, a diamond-eyed skeleton in a hooded cloak, and a magic sorceress holding a fiery crystal sun high above her head.

"They're all safe!" Todd exclaims with relief. He helps you put them back and closes the box.

"But we're not safe!" you say.

*Turn to PAGE 121 and see why.*

"Well," you hear your mom saying as you inch closer to her, "I just think we're awfully lucky to have such good kids. It's nice to know we can always trust them to do the right thing."

*The right thing. The right thing. The right thing.* Your mother's voice echoes in your head.

"Don't listen to her!" the troll cries. He pops into view and stands on a hat rack next to you. "I am your master now!" he shouts. "You will obey me!"

"Yes, Master," you reply. It's useless to argue. You have no super-strength when it comes to fighting off the will of the troll.

The troll orders you to search the library. The box could be buried under books. You sneak past the card players. The library door has a giant padlock on it. You can't budge it.

I could really use those super-strength muscles now, you think.

*Will your wish be granted? Find out on PAGE 5.*

You feel your brain magically power up. Facts pour out of your mouth like a fountain of knowledge gone wild.

"On May 20, 1927, Charles Lindbergh started his flight across the Atlantic," you announce. "The first African-American Supreme Court Justice, Thurgood Marshall, was born on July 2, 1908. Wolfgang Amadeus Mozart composed more than six hundred works of music!"

Lauren is amazed! "You know everything!" she exclaims. "But what should we do about the werewolves?"

Your brain is already solving that problem. You know you could feed them the Cherry-O's and that might calm them. But you have a different idea this time.

*Go to PAGE 122.*

"No, really," Lauren insists. "I mean Todd's body is now the size of a thimble, and he has a fish head instead of his own head! He really does look funny!"

"Come to think of it, Lauren, you're not looking too normal yourself!" Todd says through his new fish lips.

Sure enough, Lauren and you and Todd ate from the right pocket, which turns out to have been the absolute *wrong* pocket. That wasn't SUPER-STRENGTH O's you ate. It was FISH-IN-AN-INSTANT food!

Never trust a troll. They're always up to something fishy, especially when they live by a lake.

"Time to go swimming, my fine finned friends," the troll announces, as he pops out from under the stairs. He nods his head and magically transports the three of you to the middle of Deep Woods Lake. Sad to say, when it comes to fish tales, you'll be the greatest tale ever told!

**THE END**

# 128

You decide to break through the wall. You take two steps backward. Then with a running dive, you throw all your muscles against the wall. *CRRAASSSSSH!* You did it! You're back in the library.

"Uh-oh. Looks like troll trouble again!" you say. The wastebasket is tipped over and the heavy dictionary is on the floor. The troll is nowhere in sight. He has escaped!

*Tweeeeeeeeeeeet!* That awful whistle again!

The troll is in here somewhere, you guess. You hurry to the card room where your parents were. Card games are left unfinished. Cards are scattered all over the table. Half-eaten sandwiches and drinks are everywhere. Your Walkman is on the table where your dad was sitting. You pick it up. Dad never would have left it behind unless he left in a hurry, you think. The troll must have done something to them! I've got to save Mom and Dad before it's too late!

You head for the snack bar room. You open the door and gasp.

*Go to PAGE 83.*

The werewolf pounces on Lauren.

You scream. Todd screams. And Lauren . . .

. . . laughs!

"Hey, that tickles!" She giggles as she rolls on the ground with the werewolf. Her eyes aren't covered anymore. "Wolfie, stop!"

"Wolfie?" you and Todd repeat together.

You can't figure out what she means. The smartness from the cereal must have worn off. Why in the world would she be laughing?

You shine the flashlight on the werewolf. It's licking, not biting, Lauren's face.

"This isn't a werewolf," Lauren says. And in the light from the flashlight you see Lauren is right. It's not a werewolf at all.

"Wolfie is the dog from next door!" Lauren explains, hugging the hairy animal.

Oh well, so much for the great wild werewolf you were going to capture and donate to science. Good-bye to all those brilliant ideas. It looks like your chance to be famous just came to

**THE END**

You have entered the Tunnel of the Wolves.

Now you hear a bone-chilling *HOW-OW-OW-OWL!*

Again. *HOW-OW-OW-OWL!* Only this time it isn't exactly bone-chilling. It sounds more like chalk screeching on a blackboard.

"I don't think that's a werewolf howl," you say aloud. Then you see a very surprising sight.

It's Todd! He looks awful. His hair is covered in slime dropped by the slugs on the cave's ceiling. His geeky face is completely white, and his mouth is wide open in a howling O-shape.

"Todd!" you shout, startling him out of his howling. "Are you totally nuts, or what? What are you doing?"

"I'm making the werewolves think I'm one of them," Todd answers in a terrified and shaky voice. "I heard them running! I didn't know what to do, so I started howling."

"I don't believe it," you say. "Todd, you are —"

Then you hear the werewolves, too. They're running. But which way? Toward you or away from you?

*Go to PAGE 68.*

Quickly, you duck into the library. Your giant muscles make it easy for you to put the door back into the doorway. No one can even see that it was removed. You hear your parents' voices outside the door. You want to answer. The troll appears on a table next to you.

"Do not reveal your master!" he snaps.

You can see that the troll is getting ready to whistle and make your muscles disappear. Before he has the chance to pucker up his fat lips, you pick up a wastebasket. You throw the basket over the troll. Then you plop a heavy dictionary on top of the basket to hold it down.

The whistling begins. You feel yourself weakening just a little. You lean against a bookshelf. Without warning, the wall of books begins to move! The next thing you know you're standing on the other side of the wall!

*Go to PAGE 74.*

# 132

You hear the noise again. And then you spot a person hiding in the shadows of an evergreen tree.

"W-who's there?" you stutter. You shine your flashlight toward the person's face.

"Lauren!" you cry. "What are you doing out here so late?"

Lauren Woods squints into the glare of the flashlight. "Hey! Get that light out of my eyes!" she calls. You point the beam of light at the ground, as Lauren steps out from behind the tree.

"I saw weird lights blinking outside my cabin window. I decided to investigate," Lauren explains. "What about you? Why are you creeping around the woods at night?"

"The Murphy brothers stole Todd's red tin box with his pewter figure collection in it," you tell her. You introduce Lauren to Todd, and then continue. "We're out looking for it."

"I'll help," Lauren volunteers. "Let's just hope we find the box and not the Murphys! They're bigger and meaner than — ooops!"

Lauren trips on something and grabs onto Todd. Todd reaches out for you. Like dominoes, you all fall down in a line. Your flashlight shines on a mound of freshly dug dirt. You glance around. There are *a lot* of piles of dirt.

"Hey," you say. "Either we've landed in a gopher's paradise, or someone has buried something here. Let's start digging!"

*Go to PAGE 110.*

Quickly, you duck down behind an old tree stump. You listen for the footsteps again. They're closer now. But in the darkness you can't tell exactly where they are coming from.

Your heart pounds like a jackhammer.

Footsteps.

Closer, closer, closer.

"AAAAaaahhhhhh!" you scream. A hand is on your shoulder! You're afraid to look!

"Hey, hey! What do you say?" Todd's voice breaks through your scream. "It's just me. I came out to find you. After all, it's my box and I should help you find it."

You can't believe this guy! He just scared you out of your wits! And he's still talking about that stupid box!

You catch your breath and try to slow your heartbeat down to normal. "Get a life, Todd!" you snap at him. "You shouldn't sneak up on me like that!"

"I just want to help find the box," Todd whines. "Look — I even brought a flashlight!"

You're glad it's Todd and not a werewolf. In fact, you're glad for any company on a night like this. "Follow me," you say.

"Which way?" Todd asks.

*Go to PAGE 75.*

# About the Author

R.L. STINE is the most popular author in America. Recent titles for teenagers include *I Saw You That Night!*, *Call Waiting*, *Halloween Night II*, *The Dead Girlfriend*, and *The Baby-sitter IV*, all published by Scholastic. He is also the author of the *Fear Street* series.

Bob lives in New York City with his wife, Jane, and teenage son, Matt.

# GET
# Goosebumps®
## by R.L. Stine

| | | | |
|---|---|---|---|
| ☐ BAB45365-3 | #1 | Welcome to Dead House | $3.99 |
| ☐ BAB45366-1 | #2 | Stay Out of the Basement | $3.99 |
| ☐ BAB45367-X | #3 | Monster Blood | $3.99 |
| ☐ BAB45368-8 | #4 | Say Cheese and Die! | $3.99 |
| ☐ BAB45369-6 | #5 | The Curse of the Mummy's Tomb | $3.99 |
| ☐ BAB45370-X | #6 | Let's Get Invisible! | $3.99 |
| ☐ BAB46617-8 | #7 | Night of the Living Dummy | $3.99 |
| ☐ BAB46618-6 | #8 | The Girl Who Cried Monster | $3.99 |
| ☐ BAB46619-4 | #9 | Welcome to Camp Nightmare | $3.99 |
| ☐ BAB49445-7 | #10 | The Ghost Next Door | $3.99 |
| ☐ BAB49446-5 | #11 | The Haunted Mask | $3.99 |
| ☐ BAB49447-3 | #12 | Be Careful What You Wish for... | $3.99 |
| ☐ BAB49448-1 | #13 | Piano Lessons Can Be Murder | $3.99 |
| ☐ BAB49449-x | #14 | The Werewolf of Fever Swamp | $3.99 |
| ☐ BAB49450-3 | #15 | You Can't Scare Me! | $3.99 |
| ☐ BAB47738-2 | #16 | One Day at HorrorLand | $3.99 |
| ☐ BAB47739-0 | #17 | Why I'm Afraid of Bees | $3.99 |
| ☐ BAB47740-4 | #18 | Monster Blood II | $3.99 |
| ☐ BAB47741-2 | #19 | Deep Trouble | $3.99 |
| ☐ BAB47742-0 | #20 | The Scarecrow Walks at Midnight | $3.99 |
| ☐ BAB47743-9 | #21 | Go Eat Worms! | $3.99 |
| ☐ BAB47744-7 | #22 | Ghost Beach | $3.99 |
| ☐ BAB47745-5 | #23 | Return of the Mummy | $3.99 |
| ☐ BAB48354-4 | #24 | Phantom of the Auditorium | $3.99 |
| ☐ BAB48355-2 | #25 | Attack of the Mutant | $3.99 |
| ☐ BAB48350-1 | #26 | My Hairiest Adventure | $3.99 |
| ☐ BAB48351-X | #27 | A Night in Terror Tower | $3.99 |
| ☐ BAB48352-8 | #28 | The Cuckoo Clock of Doom | $3.99 |
| ☐ BAB48347-1 | #29 | Monster Blood III | $3.99 |
| ☐ BAB48348-X | #30 | It Came from Beneath the Sink | $3.99 |
| ☐ BAB48349-8 | #31 | The Night of the Living Dummy II | $3.99 |
| ☐ BAB48344-7 | #32 | The Barking Ghost | $3.99 |
| ☐ BAB48345-5 | #33 | The Horror at Camp Jellyjam | $3.99 |
| ☐ BAB48346-3 | #34 | Revenge of the Lawn Gnomes | $3.99 |
| ☐ BAB48340-4 | #35 | A Shocker on Shock Street | $3.99 |
| ☐ BAB56873-6 | #36 | The Haunted Mask II | $3.99 |
| ☐ BAB56874-4 | #37 | The Headless Ghost | $3.99 |

| | | | |
|---|---|---|---|
| ❏ BAB56875-2 | #38 | The Abominable Snowman of Pasadena | $3.99 |
| ❏ BAB56876-0 | #39 | How I Got My Shrunken Head | $3.99 |
| ❏ BAB56877-9 | #40 | Night of the Living Dummy III | $3.99 |
| ❏ BAB56878-7 | #41 | Bad Hare Day | $3.99 |
| ❏ BAB56879-5 | #42 | Egg Monsters from Mars | $3.99 |
| ❏ BAB56644-X | | Goosebumps 1996 Calendar | $9.95 |
| ❏ BAB62836-4 | | Book & Light Set #1: Tales to Give You Goosebumps | $11.95 |
| ❏ BAB26603-9 | | Book & Light Set #2: More Tales to Give You Goosebumps | $11.95 |
| ❏ BAB55323-2 | | Give Yourself Goosebumps Book #1: Escape from the Carnival of Horrors | $3.99 |
| ❏ BAB56645-8 | | Give Yourself Goosebumps Book #2: Tick Tock, You're Dead | $3.99 |
| ❏ BAB56646-6 | | Give Yourself Goosebumps Book #3: Trapped in Bat Wing Hall | $3.99 |
| ❏ BAB67318-1 | | Give Yourself Goosebumps Book #4: The Deadly Experiments of Dr. Eeek | $3.99 |
| ❏ BAB67319-X | | Give Yourself Goosebumps Book #5: Night in Werewolf Woods | $3.99 |
| ❏ BAB53770-9 | | The Goosebumps Monster Blood Pack | $11.95 |
| ❏ BAB50995-0 | | The Goosebumps Monster Edition #1 | $12.95 |
| ❏ BAB60265-9 | | Goosebumps Official Collector's Caps Collecting Kit | $5.99 |

------------------------------------------------------------------

### Scare me, thrill me, mail me GOOSEBUMPS now!

Available wherever you buy books, or use this order form. Scholastic Inc., P.O. Box 7502,
2931 East McCarty Street, Jefferson City, MO 65102

Please send me the books I have checked above. I am enclosing $_____ (please add
$2.00 to cover shipping and handling). Send check or money order — no cash or C.O.D.s please.

Name _____Age _____

Address _____

City _____State/Zip _____

Please allow four to six weeks for delivery. Offer good in the U.S. only. Sorry, mail orders are not available to
residents of Canada. Prices subject to change.

GB995

# Every Beast for Himself!

# Goosebumps®

Ginger Wald and her identical twin
brothers, Nat and Pat, are lost in the
woods...and there's something odd going on.
The grass is yellow, the bushes are purple,
and the trees are like skyscrapers.
Then Ginger and her brothers meet
the beasts... big blue furry creatures
who want to play a game.
The winners get to live.
The losers get eaten....

# The Beast from the East
## Goosebumps #43
by R.L. Stine

**Creeping into a bookstore near you!**